NEVER TO BE TOLD

Jennifer Lynch

(Copyright Jennifer Lynch 2017 all rights reserved)
Revised Version October 2022

No part of this publication may be
reproduced or transmitted by any means,
electronic, mechanical, photocopying or otherwise
without the prior permission of the publisher.,

Chapter 1 - By the Lake

Angela sat beside the lake and gazed at the water, in a long black woolen coat, scarf, and gloves. She was trying to keep warm on a freezing cold winter's day. Most of the lake was covered with ice, but as the sun sparkled on the water, it was gradually melting, creating an area where the ducks could swim. She pulled her scarf tightly around her and breathed in deeply. Feeding ducks was always therapeutic. Angela had enjoyed doing it with her children when they were young, and although she was alone today, there was something special about watching them taking her bread.

Despite the cold, Angela enjoyed visiting the lake. She reflected on how quickly the years had passed. It felt like only yesterday, when her two young children were with her, and they were now both teenagers. Still, the ducks needed feeding, especially on a day like today. She decided to try to visit more often because the silence was calming. She quickly took out some bread from the carrier bag she'd grabbed this morning, and broke it into pieces. When the bread had gone, she noticed a family a few meters away throwing food. The children looked excited and shouted, "quick, give me more." They'll be well fed today, she thought.

It was Valentine's Day 2008, and there was no valentine card this morning, but as there was no-one special in her life, she wasn't expecting one. About a month or so ago, she'd ended her relationship with Martin, the Head of the School, where she worked as a teacher. She was relieved their relationship was over because it was stressful and it wasn't going anywhere. So today, a walk, a cup of tea and cake would be better than procrastinating over her love life.

The lake looked beautiful this morning. Angela noticed the bare branches of the trees with the vast sky above. She loved this about Suffolk, being able to see so much of the sky. Despite the cold wind, the sun sparkled generously on the water, creating what resembled a collection of diamonds. I couldn't ask for a better Valentine's gift than this, she whispered, feeling happy in her own company.

Angela stood up from a wooden seat, feeling slightly damp and began to walk briskly to warm her body. She started to observe the skyline, rather than noticing the muddy path beneath her feet. In recent years, efforts had been made to add shingle for bikes and wheelchairs but it had rained heavily in recent weeks and the layer of mud which covered the surface had turned into ice. She wound her way along the tree-lined path, and reflected on a Valentine's Day when she'd received a beautiful bunch of roses from her husband. It was a rare occurrence during their marriage, but it had made her happy. However, only a few days later, the rose heads drooped, and despite giving them a little lemonade to perk them up, the roses, like her marriage never recovered. Their feelings for each other also diminished, and it was beyond repair. It was a sad time in her life, but it was the past, and Angela wanted to leave it there. Today was a new day, and she had to make the best of it. She tried to live her life with a full cup, and although she sometimes reflected on the past, it was seldom for long.

Angela was now forty-five years old, but she looked at least eight years younger, being fit and having a slim figure. She worked as a Sports Teacher at Cherryfields School, which was only a few miles from her home. Angela enjoyed some aspects of her job, but the working hours took up nearly all her time. Despite this, she still managed to squeeze in some occasional runs and sessions at the gym. Her friends couldn't understand why she was still on her own. Being single was partly her choice because she hadn't been particularly good at relationships in the past and had lost the will to try. She'd dated a few men since her divorce in 2000, but none of them had turned in to anything. Her relationship with Martin was more about lust from the start and she knew it wouldn't change.

Angela frequently declared that she'd never been in love. During her marriage to Chris, she'd experienced a type of love, which she now realised was co-dependency. Chris had always put her on a pedestal, and she fell below his expectations, which were based on his relationship with his mother. The woman he wanted didn't exist. Still, despite his ideals, he chose to finish their relationship. Some weeks later, Angela discovered that he'd been having an affair with his new secretary, Monica, which came as a shock.

Monica was a smart young woman, who wore her hair up in a bun. When Chris first talked about her, Angela thought she sounded like a woman from a 1950's television advertisement. Her twee clothes and her restored Morris Miner, conjured up an image of a suppressed woman who couldn't say boo to a goose. When she'd met her at a work's meal, she couldn't believe how self-contained she was. Chris often talked about her and said that she was easy going and fun. Perhaps she'd judged her unfairly because whatever his attraction was for her, she didn't understand it? When Angela's relationship with Chris finally ended, he explained to her that his affair with Monica had never been sexual. It was more an affair of the heart. But Angela wasn't sure if that was better or worse, part of her wanted Chris to have had a sexual relationship with her so she could feel angry. She tried to walk away with her head held high, saying, it wasn't her fault. If only life were that simple. An affair of the heart was sad because she knew they'd stopped listening to each other and they were both lonely. Once the conversation had gone, the roses also went, and no sweet words were going to bring their relationship back to life.

Angela couldn't believe how quickly her love affair

with Martin had developed, but she guessed it was because she was vulnerable. It just sneaked up on her. Months later, when it became apparent that Martin wasn't the man for her, she decided to focus her attention on her career and helping her sons to achieve their dreams. She was determined they'd both have good jobs and security in their lives.

Deep in thought, Angela continued to follow a small stream, which gently meandered from the lake to an adjoining meadow. The little creek was full to brimming point, and she was surprised it was gushing. The path quickly turned into a slippery track, which she could still walk along if she took it slowly. She was glad that she'd worn her walking boots which made things easier. Angela knew that it wouldn't be long before snowdrops and crocuses appeared along the banks of the stream, which was something she looked forward to. She felt as if this winter had gone on forever, and she wanted the warm weather to come so she could run again. She found it hard to keep fit during the winter months, and she couldn't afford to let her fitness routine slide.

Angela suddenly felt a tap on the back of her shoulder. She'd been so deep in thought she jumped then, quickly spun around to see who it was. She was angry that someone had approached her from behind.

"You've dropped a glove?" said the voice.

A man stood in front of her holding the glove out. She quickly took it realising it must have fallen out of her pocket, perhaps through searching for a tissue. She had a slight cold today, but it didn't deter her from coming to the lake. She was surprised that she hadn't heard the man walk up behind her, but she'd been deep in thought. Her friends often said that she was away with the fairies and they were right.

The man was tall, dark and in an unusual way, good looking. Although his face was strained with worry. Smiling would make him more appealing, she thought, as she met his gaze.

"Thanks, I didn't realise I'd dropped it!" she said, giving him a little smile. As he went to walk away, he suddenly hesitated and said "you'll need that today because it's cold. I didn't have time to get bread for the ducks. Have you got any?"

He lingered a while, waiting for her to answer, then smiled.

Angela was right about the smile because it transformed his face, and she immediately felt an attraction towards him. She knew the appeal was happening far too quickly, but deep down, Angela was a true romantic. After all it was Valentine's Day. Surely, she was allowed a little flirt?

"Yes, I've fed them already, but you can get bread at the shop. It's only a short walk," she replied in a friendly manner.

"I haven't got much time today, so I think I'll just walk. By the way, my name's Gareth, and you are?"

"I'm Angela, pleased to meet you. Yes, it's cold, and it's best to keep moving. I want to get to the cafe soon because I'm going to town this afternoon. The shops shut early on Sundays. It's mad because people need them to be open longer."

"Yes, I agree. The cafe, where's that?" asked Gareth, sounding interested.

"It's a fifteen-minute walk from here, down the other end of the lake," said Angela as she started to walk away.

"Well, ok, I may as well come with you because my boys are still playing football," said Gareth, smiling. Angela smiled back and nodded.

He seemed pleasant enough, and she thought that she might enjoy his company.

As they reached the cafe, she noticed two magpies sitting on top of the cafe's adjoining fence, which were very still.

"Now we're here, I'd love a cuppa because I'm frozen. Do you mind if I keep you company a while longer?" he asked.

Angela thought for a moment. She realised he was a stranger, but he'd been kind enough to return her glove, so why not. It could be fun to spend a little time with someone new.

"Yes sure, but I'm not going to be here long though because I've got to get home to sort my sons out."

"Sort them out? How old are they?"

"Teenagers", she replied, and he nodded while glancing at his watch.

"Look at those two magpies on that fence. They look like they're chatting away with each other. It's unusual because I haven't seen them before."

"What you've never seen Magpies, before?" he said, sounding surprised.

"Yes, of course, I've seen Magpies before, but I've never seen two of them sitting there."

"Magpies are strange birds and who knows what they hoard. They're a law unto themselves. This looks like a great place, Angela. Where would you like to sit?" asked Gareth, looking around. They decided to sit in the corner, near the window, so that they could still see the lake. Angela looked out and noticed the magpies had flown from the fence.

The lake looked more enchanting than when she first arrived. The more the sun came out, the quicker the ice melted. It had almost completely disappeared, apart from in the shade where it clung to the edges.

"I work in the city. I commute to work, which can be a bit of a pain. I love Suffolk, and I wouldn't give it up. Working in London is great, but living there is another story. I used to live in North London a few years ago, but now everything's changed, and rents are sky-high. It's become a trendy area to live, although London is still London! Who wouldn't prefer the countryside with its big green spaces, trees, and lakes. It's a gift!"

"I agree", replied Angela, not wanting to reveal too much about herself. At the same time, she realised that there was something about Gareth that intrigued her. A group of young people in sports clothes walked into the cafe to join the queue. Gareth looked at them. "They look like they ran here," he said.

"I run," Angela said, thinking it sounded slightly bizarre, but he looked at her and smiled. She didn't want to tell him that she was a sports teacher in case it sounded dull.

"That's sporty of you Angela. How far do you go?" he continued.

"I normally run around 5K most days, but not when it's this cold. I decided to walk today because it's icy. I also wanted to treat myself because ..." she ran out of words.

"Because what?" Gareth urged her to continue, then, finished her sentence. "Because it's Valentine's Day, isn't it? Yes, I almost forgot. I suppose that's why there's a red rose in each vase?" he said, looking around the cafe, smirking.

Angela ignored his smirk. She loved Reed Rush Cafe. It had sprung to life a few years ago, and it was always packed out on Sundays. Today was no exception, and they were lucky to find a table. The staff rushed around clearing tables, getting them ready for more people who had begun to queue outside.

To the side of the cafe, there was a large farm shop and a couple of quaint little gift shops. Gareth said he didn't know it existed until today. Angela was surprised by this because he said he was a frequent visitor to the lake, but he'd never bothered to walk this far? Perhaps he usually sat in his car on his mobile. A lot of people did that!

Gareth was amazed by how busy it was and how

great the food looked, and they decided to order some cakes.

"There's a good selection of food here, brilliant. I'll come again," he said enthusiastically.

Fortunately, they only had to wait for a short time before they were served, having got in just before the runners. The waitress then brought over their tea and said that she'd return with their cakes shortly.

"They must have a real rush on today because you'd normally have your cakes with your tea, not afterwards", said Angela, feeling slightly disgruntled.

"I don't mind waiting because this is such a nice place," said Gareth looking around at the pine tables and red checked table cloths. "It's a very, attractive barn, isn't it? It's around three hundred years old. You won't find anything like this in London. Or if you did, it would be too expensive to eat there."

Angela was fascinated by Gareth's slow and steady speech which held her attention. She'd consider him eloquent if it wasn't for his long fringe which he regularly swept back from his face. Angela thought he would benefit from a haircut, but Gareth loved it. It gave him an edge. As he talked about his work and golf, she noticed the strain vanish. It must be good for him to get away from his work in the city, she thought. She was pleased when the cakes finally arrived which looked delicious.

"I always have a couple of hours to kill on Sundays, while my boys play football. I used to watch them but they found my clapping and cheering embarrassing, so I eventually got the message and decided to walk around the lake instead. It's so peaceful, and it helps me unwind. Do you mind if I smoke Angela, now we've finished?" he asked.

"Ok, but we'll have to sit outside," she replied.

Angela wasn't pleased with Gareth's smoking. Her ex-husband Chris used to smoke, which she hated because health, was her middle name. But because she wanted to spend more time with him, she followed him out.

"So, you're single then?" he asked, looking her straight in the eyes. I bet you received a card or two today?" he continued with a cheeky grin.

Angela was surprised that he said that. She wanted to say, 'you're a cheeky devil, that's personal, but she grinned because she was flattered.

"I had a couple. How about you?" she replied.

"Oh dozens," he said, laughing. Angela noticed that Gareth looked very comfortable and she started to relax. "Last time I had a card was a long time ago because I've been on my own for a while now. It's given me the chance to catch up with myself and to enjoy life. I love playing golf when I'm not working, but with looking after my sons some weekends, I don't have much time for hobbies." He explained.

"Yes, I know that one," Angela sighed. "I have to go soon, or I'll miss the shops. She quickly glanced down at her mobile and decided to make a move. Shaun needed to be at his friend's by 2 pm, then, she'd promised to pop into town with Marcus. She also had a load of other jobs to finish before they left.

"Well, it's been great talking to you Gareth," she

said as she went to stand up.

"Yes, me too, it's been great talking to you, Angela. Please take my card so we can keep in touch?" he said, giving her a proper smile.

Angela promptly took his card.

"Call me," he said, as he hurried away in the direction of the car park. Angela noticed that he looked at his watch before disappearing.

Angela knew that they'd made a great connection. Her immediate attraction was something she hadn't experienced since she met Martin. She was now sure that her relationship with him was over, even though she knew he still fancied her. How could that relationship ever be right for her when he would never tell her the truth? She needed someone available, and Gareth appeared to be that. However, this time she was going to avoid assumptions because they'd always led her on pointless diversions. Maybe if she asked the right questions from the start, it would be plain sailing?

Chapter 2 – Rainy Mondays!

Monday morning came, and it was raining and cold. Angela pulled into the school's staff car park to park in her usual spot. She was early, so she decided to check her handbag to make sure everything was in place for her day. Angela planned to go shopping after work and her purse was often in strange places. As she searched in her bag, she suddenly noticed Gareth's business card at the bottom. There was his business number and above that, was Gareth Jones, Architect, 783 Winston House, Islington, London. She quickly returned it to her bag, because right now, she was more concerned about Martin.

Things had become increasingly tense between them since she told him they were over, a few months ago. She knew that ultimately, there was no way to avoid him because he was the Head of Cherryfields and their professional relationship was at stake. How could she opt-out of their staff meetings and appraisals because it was part of her job? So, for the foreseeable future, she knew that she would still see him regularly and she'd just have to put up with it however much it irritated her. She thought he always looked slightly smug about their intimate relationship, which upset her because what had happened between them was in the past, and he needed to wipe that smirk off his face. She was certainly strong enough now not to be pulled back into that relationship. For one, it was not fair on her and two, it wasn't fair on his wife. They'd had some fun dates and also spent some nights together. Either at Angela's house when her sons were away or at a hotel. Martin always felt guilty afterwards, and he'd burden her with it, which was something that she'd never been happy with. It was his choice if he wanted to be unfaithful to his wife. His marital problems weren't her concern. Over the few months they were together, it became increasingly clear to her that Martin had no intention of leaving his wife, despite his promises. He wanted to play with women from a position of comfort. Why didn't he face the fact that his marriage was over, because it was evident to Angela that there was nothing between them? Martin said that she hadn't been interested in sex since the birth of their last child, ten years ago. He said it wasn't a proper marriage, but Angela knew as Martin wasn't divorced, or separated he wasn't available. He was still married even if the sexual side of his relationship was over. He'd also showed her some property particulars of a house he was interested in renting, saying that his wife could carry on living in the family home until the children left. As time went on, Angela realised Martin exaggerated his domestic circumstances and his words sounded like a sob story. She felt compassion but annoyed that he couldn't front up to his wife. He was lying to

Jackie because he no longer loved her and he was sexually attracted to other women. Angela knew she wasn't the first woman that he'd had an affair with because he was very experienced in bed. She didn't want to boost his ego by telling him how amazing he was because she sensed he was looking for admiration and power. Even though Angela had seen behind his mask, she couldn't deny that he was a fantastic lover. He'd spent many hours making sure that she felt comfortable with him before they went to bed, getting her relaxed before they made love. By the time they got into bed, she felt as if she was bursting, calling out his name over and over. Martin loved Angela's name-calling. The realisation that she desired him made him feel like a God. This was something that he'd never experienced with Jackie, and he was attracted to Angela like a magnet. He wanted to please her so that he could be adored. He stroked her gently, as if she was a young child, having great patience with her. He took his time making love to her, not neglecting any part of her body. He stroked her hair, her face, touched each finger and toe, which made her feel special and loved. She was his fragile doll who couldn't be broken. Yet, Angela knew he didn't love her because he was in love with himself and his performance. Martin knew the effect he had on her. He wanted her to talk about her desires, to live out her fantasies and be part of his self-made movie. He also wanted her to bare her soul by revealing her deepest secrets. She knew that some women would find his lovemaking incredible.

His mental-probing being as deep as his physicality, but after a few months, Angela began to notice a darker side of Martin. It was as if he had hidden things that, he clearly didn't want her to see. It was always about her fantasies and not his. He was too eager to please, but to Angela, it was vanity. Martin had become a man looking at his own reflection. She soon realised that he had very minimal feelings for her, or for his wife, which disgusted her, but it didn't stop her desire. The man had got under her skin, and Angela realised their relationship had turned into a sexual obsession. It was defiant and she was angry for allowing it because she'd denied herself love. All this for another woman's husband? Her thoughts quickly returned to the present because there was a short staff meeting at break time. There was no way of escaping him today so she'd have to cope with it, however uncomfortable she felt.

A few weeks ago, Angela considered looking for a new position, but she knew that it wouldn't be easy to find the right location, salary, and job, which matched her skill set. She concluded that if she ignored Martin as much as possible, eventually he'd get the message she was no longer interested in him. Re-entering any type of relationship with him would be self-sabotage, and it would hurt. She would find a man who could give her the love she deserved. Until then, she would keep working on honouring herself. If this meant going without sex, then so be it. It had been the case for many years on and off. It would be how it was again, but for now, she'd enjoy her independence. Her sons were a little older now, and they were busy with their own lives. She had a lot of freedom because both of them enjoyed sport which meant that they were frequently out of the house, especially during the summer. They were either playing cricket, tennis, or out with friends.

Angela sat down at her desk, she needed to organise this afternoon's lessons. Monday was her free morning which meant there weren't any lessons until after lunch, so today was about planning and getting through the national curriculum.

The meeting at break time was about the appointment of a new deputy head. Martin wanted to keep his staff in the loop about who he was taking on and why. The candidates were interviewed a week ago, and now it was crunch time. The current deputy head had already left. He'd been a heavy drinker, and he spent more time worrying about when and where he was going to have his next drink, than teaching. His organisational skills had severely suffered, and when Martin finally got to the bottom of what was going on, it was impossible to keep Jerry on. The children teased him in class because he frequently stumbled, and he wasn't in control of his lessons. It was unfortunate, but he had to go.

The bell rang, and Angela headed to the staff room. She felt exhausted and wanted to slump into the nearest chair. If only today could be over. She noticed Martin standing at his filing cabinet collating the relevant documents for the meeting. She regretted being slightly early because they were alone.

"Hey, Angela, you look tired. What did you do at the weekend? Out clubbing I suppose or up all night with some man?"

Angela just glared at him. She wasn't impressed. She didn't want to take the bait and enter into a conversation just before a meeting. Martin had a nasty way of putting her down, and he was waiting for a reaction. It may have been just a joke to him, but she didn't like it because he was mocking her. That was Martin's way; to mock and call it a joke. It was very immature for a man in his fifties. Then, he'd make a move on her when she was vulnerable. Well, she wasn't vulnerable now, and she didn't need him. She didn't want to know anything about him, his intelligence, his smile, his attitude, or his body. She turned her head away, but he continued to stare at her. He wasn't going to let the conversation drop until he found out how she'd spent her weekend.

"I don't know why you're interested, Martin, but as you asked, I was busy with my sons, and I went to watch a rugby match, ok?"

"I'm always interested in you Angela, you know that," Martin said, smiling. The problem is that you make me feel so horny I want to..."

The door swung open, and the rest of the staff suddenly walked in. Angela sat up in her chair and tried to pull herself together. She didn't care whether Martin wanted to fuck her or not, as he was about to say. She didn't want him. He needed to sort out his relationship with his wife. It was probably his fault anyway. She didn't know if she had ever believed the 'I haven't had sex since the birth of our child story.' The man was full of excuses and exaggerations.

He handed her a pile of papers to pass to the rest of the staff. She cringed and then gave the documents to her colleagues. She noticed that the appointment of the Deputy Head had moved to item one on the agenda, which she was somewhat surprised at.

Mike, the music teacher, also looked surprised and said, "Martin, I don't know why discussing the new Deputy Head is now item number one? I thought that we'd already discussed that at our last meeting and we'd all agreed on Stuart?"

Martin stood up and paced around the staff room. He looked very uncomfortable being put on the spot, and he cleared his throat.

"Well, although I initially thought that Stuart would make the best Deputy Head, after much contemplation, I've realised that Sally's credentials more accurately fit the post. Her C.V. was brilliant, and she interviewed exceptionally well, plus having another female member of staff, will balance things out a little.

Unusually, there was a deathly hush in the room. Then, Martin began to cough. It was apparent to Angela that he was finding it hard to explain his actions. What was going on? Surely, he wasn't choosing the candidate by their sex? But who could argue when both of the candidates were suitable?

Mike suddenly leaned forward and whispered into her ear.

"I bet she's got big boobs!"

"Yes, I would imagine so," replied Angela feeling a little sick.

She wished that she wasn't at this meeting this morning, it was unbearable. Martin was so predictable that it made her angry. She turned her attention to the window sill because there was a slight tapping noise. To her surprise, a Magpie was pecking at the glass. No-one else was aware of it, so she decided to keep quiet. She stared at the bird for a few moments, and she swore that the Magpie stared back at her! It then flew away as quickly as it had landed.

"Don't you agree, Angela?" she suddenly heard Martin say.

"Do I agree with what? Ah yes, perfect." she said slightly sarcastically, showing little interest in Martin's views. She knew that he was well on his way to luring another woman. Her credentials, she had a titter. Why did he do this? She suddenly felt sorry for his wife, which surprised her. Her relationship with Martin had brought her to a new understanding. Someone ought to tell her the truth, she thought. She took a large swig of water in the hope that it might wake her up enough to focus on what was being said, but Angela knew she'd switched off and it would take a bolt of lightning to engage her. She glanced at Martin's desk. The desk where they'd first had sex together. It had happened late one evening when she'd stayed behind to help him finish some work, and before she knew it, he was as he put it 'fucking her on his desk!' At first, she wanted him to stop. Not because she didn't fancy him because there was a strong sexual attraction, but because she knew he was married. He'd even put down a blanket on top of the desk so that they'd be comfortable, how considerate! Angela had no idea what was coming next, but as she went to remove the blanket, Martin slid his hands around her waist and pressed himself against her.

Angela didn't particularly enjoy their encounter. Part of her felt that it was exciting, and made her heart race, but another part of her felt cheap. It was also extremely uncomfortable, despite the blanket. She then decided to keep away from him for weeks. He knew she was avoiding him, and he eventually asked her out to dinner. No doubt his desk would be used again, she thought, as she took her attention away from it. She'd have to develop a mental rubber to rub out the image of them together. It was going to be a lot easier now since she'd met the man at the lake!

Chapter 3 – Martin's Game

Unfortunately, Angela was not history to Martin. He was aware of his sexual hold on her, and he kept trying to play his trump card. It would take patience, but he had all the time in the world and was happy to wait. If only he could convince her that he was serious about leaving his wife. He would be back in the game. He wished that he had married a woman like her, but those women were hard to find. Angela was sexy, sporty and intelligent which was an attractive combination. She'd also made him feel young and fertile, unlike his wife, who made him feel old. Jackie always suffered from bad headaches, and they'd slept in separate bedrooms for years. He knew his she was no longer attracted to him. Something had died between them after the birth of their last child. It was a complicated birth, after which Jackie suffered a long period of depression. Martin had done his best to support her, but she'd never returned that support. Pleasing him in bed was supporting him, so why wouldn't she do that? He was still young enough to enjoy sex and he didn't want that part of his life to be over when he was only in his fifties. She left him no option but to find lovers who didn't mind him being married! In the beginning, he experienced a lot of guilt about his affairs, but as time went on, he justified his actions, and any negative thoughts vanished.

Angela was the best lover that he'd ever had. He knew that he'd messed it up by saying that he was leaving Jackie and not following through. How could he leave her when he loved her? The fact that they no longer had sex together didn't stop him from loving her. She was the mother of his children, and she'd worked hard. She was also a teacher who taught English at a nearby comprehensive school. Martin thought that it was just as well they didn't work together because he needed his space. His constant parent and school governor meetings allowed him the time to slip in a few extracurricular activities. This was when he met his lovers. The women he drew were lonely, vulnerable and missed sex. He often described them as hungry for sex. Sex was love for Martin. He knew that he'd never be able to give these women what they wanted; a serious commitment but the relationships were filling a void. Sally was the ideal new Deputy Head. She had precisely the right experience for the job. Hopefully, with her working knowledge, she'd help him turn the school around. They'd need regular meetings together to discuss his ideas. They could start by tackling the smoking issues during lunchtime. Martin needed help to engage these kids because some of them appeared to have lost it. They had very little focus and behaved like they were in a trance! Mobile phones were the biggest problem. The children were so pre-occupied with them that he'd had to make a no-phone in class policy. This meant that they were only allowed to bring in their mobile if it was turned off. Despite this, he noticed that the children were still using their phones without sound, which resulted in a lack of attention. This was a big problem because they were also addicted to social media. What a nightmare.

Martin strolled towards his office window, which overlooked the vast sports field. Angela would be out there this afternoon with her class. Martin loved to see her in her shorts, demonstrating games. She seldom looked up. She was unaware of him watching her. It was stupid to waste his time watching when he had so much to do, but he passed it off as a necessary part of her assessment. He kidded himself it was his duty to observe her as headteacher, but in truth, he knew that he liked to watch Angela's toned backside running around the field because it aroused him.

Martin looked at his watch. It was twelve-thirty. He'd eat his sandwiches at one when she was out on the field. He had ten minutes to watch her, and it gave him an excuse to sit still. God, he felt horny. If he didn't shag her soon, he'd have to find someone else, and that wouldn't be easy because he didn't have the time to pursue another woman. Perhaps Sally would be someone he could get close to? The good thing about her was that she was Ms. and most likely a divorcee, which was great. Divorcees were easy to charm because they were more desperate. He thought about the shape of Sally's breasts, which he'd observed through her tight blouse. She had such beautiful eyes and gorgeous tits, which was a real turn on. During their second interview, he'd been visualising gently caressing them. He also imagined placing his mouth on hers to give her a passionate kiss. He wanted to put his tongue into her eloquent mouth to see how she tasted. He loved the taste of women. He thought it unlikely she was as gorgeous as Angela, but he also knew that he could be pleasantly surprised. He sometimes felt that he could do no better than his last lover, then along came another woman who pleased him more. Martin was looking forward to working closely with her because between them, they could get this school up and running like clockwork. They'd need to put in some extra hours, and if he were lucky, they'd have a few late evenings together.

Martin opened his desk to get out his sandwiches. He grabbed his folded picnic blanket. He covered his legs because it was cold in his office. He thought about the time that he'd had sex with Angela, on his office desk. It still made him horny every time he remembered it. He pulled the blanket further up, so it reached his waist. No-one would come in because he'd turned the sign on his door to do not disturb. He looked out of the window and saw Angela was already out on the playing field. "That woman has such a fantastic arse, he whispered". He knew that he wasn't done with her yet, but he needed to think of a new way to draw her in. Perhaps when Sally showed interest in him, it might make her want him more? He knew that she still had feelings for him, although she pretended that she didn't. No woman could turn off her feelings that quickly. Perhaps a little competition was what she needed to stoke her fire!

Chapter 4 – Family Choices

Angela felt tired. It was impossible to know which University was right for Marcus but as long as it was a good one and he liked it, she was happy. The list had to be narrowed down a little because the trips they'd selected had to fit in with her work schedule. She could take a few days holiday, but that was it. She wasn't going to let her son down, but it was hard fitting everything in. Marcus offered to get the train to some of them, but Angela wanted to look around them too. She had to know where he would spend the next three years of his life. It was vital for her and his father. It felt like a long time, three years, but Marcus would be home regularly for holidays. She knew that she needed to accept that this was the next stage of her son's life, but she couldn't help but feel a mixture of both joy and apprehension. The irony of it was that Marcus wanted to follow in her footsteps teaching sport. Angela was unhappy about this but felt a little mean. She'd tried to persuade him that there were better options. Marcus thought it made sense for him to train as a sports teacher because he loved sport and enjoyed working with children. He'd had plenty of practice over the past few years, volunteering at various summer camps, for the local leisure centre, who frequently asked for his help. Marcus was talented at football, rugby, and swimming as well as being, a born leader. He could motivate children in magical ways, so they enjoyed sport. Angela was amazed by this and deep down; she knew Marcus would make an excellent teacher. She suggested that he might like to travel for a few years. 'Why don't you go and see a little of the world before you settle into teaching', she'd told him. Her career was good. But she also felt trapped, and she didn't want Marcus to experience the same feelings. She reminded herself that he had to get his qualifications first and whatever he decided to do at university he'd have tremendous fun. But for now, he still had an awful lot of maturing ahead of him. She knew he was developing and good at making his own decisions.

Angela turned up the heating. It had been on low all day, while everyone was out, and now at 6 pm, it felt cold. She decided to get on with the dinner because they were all hungry, then she'd have time to relax. She wanted to go for a walk at the lake again soon, maybe on Sunday. She secretly hoped that she'd bump into Gareth. Angela was pleased that they both had sporty children because she knew when they met, they'd have something to talk about. Gareth's sons were a lot younger than hers but Daisy, like Marcus, would be taking her A levels this year. Gareth looked a lot younger than Martin, and he was a lot more attractive. He'd also told her that he was romantically available, which drew her. It was interesting how quickly he'd joined her on Valentine's Day. He may of course, not want to be on his own? That was the trouble with her liking men. Her constant procrastination drove her crazy. Was he like this or that? It felt a waste of time analysing him, but she couldn't help herself because part of her was already hooked on him. She felt slightly annoyed that she'd allowed that to happen after all she had only met the man once!

There was just so much to do! Not only for school, but Angela wanted to help her sons with their studies and catch up with the housework. Marcus and Shaun took care of a few things if she nagged them, but it was often more relaxed if she did it herself. Angela wondered once again if Gareth felt an attraction towards her when they first met. She wanted to slow her thoughts down and took a long deep breath because she was starting to make assumptions which were dangerous territory. Mindfulness was excellent for this. She tried to spend at least ten minutes a day, listening to an audio recording to help her gain a positive perspective. The sessions always uplifted her and things began to make more sense, plus the silence was bliss! Be mindful she repeated while she organised her home office. She knew that staying present was the key to the happiness.

Angela searched inside her handbag for Gareth's card and realised that the number was his office number and he'd probably be home by now. She quickly turned it over and saw his mobile number scribbled in pen. Angela then went upstairs to her bedroom, where it was private. It felt like a long time before he answered. Her heart was thumping, and her throat felt dry as she went to speak.

"Hi," Gareth answered.

"Hi, it's Angela," she said tentatively.

There was a long hush, and then she continued, "Angela from the lake!"

"Ah, Hi Angela, the lady of the lake/ I'm sorry, I thought for a moment you were another Angela, an old friend. How are you?" he continued not waiting for the reply. "I'm going to be down at the lake on Sunday. The kids are going to be gone for ages, so I thought that I might nip into town as well. There's a new wine bar opened near the marina called Reds if you'd like to join me?" asked Gareth

Angela was gob smacked that Gareth asked her to meet so quickly, but after a few seconds, she decided yes, she wanted to meet him, and she began to feel excited.

"Yes, that sounds good. Shall I meet you at the lake and this time you won't have to chase after me with a glove," Angela said jokingly.

"Chase you, that would be fun, but I've got a feeling that you'd easily outrun me! Great, around twelve, is perfect for me. We can go for a short walk first and then go into town for a glass of wine and a bite to eat," he answered cheerfully.

Angela was pleased that she'd found the courage, to finally call Gareth because things were turning out far better than she imagined. She now had a date with him, and she was grinning like a Cheshire cat. What on earth would she wear? Her clothes had to be suitable for walking around the lake and lunch at the wine bar, difficult!

****

Angela didn't know that time could go so slowly; she was so desperate for Sunday to arrive that when it finally came, she changed numerous times before she settled on an outfit that was both smart and casual. She still needed to do her hair, makeup and overhaul her broken nails. She'd left a strong trail of perfume lingering around the house, which her sons immediately noticed.

"Mum, it stinks of perfume." said Marcus.

"Yeah, it does. Where are you going?" asked Shaun. "I hope you'll be back later to take us to town?"

"I'm sorry, but I won't be back until around two-thirty this afternoon," Angela said, casually.

"Two-thirty," said Shaun, looking horrified, "that won't leave me enough time to look for shoes and a game before the shops close."

"Well, I'm sorry, but it's the best I can do. Or, go there by bus," said Angela, who was fed up with putting them first. They both had unhappy faces, but she knew it would pass. Her changing the pecking order would do them good. Angela grinned, then, said, "I'll be back as soon as I can, but sorry, I've got plans today. She knew that they'd be fine on their own because they were always busy with their friends at the weekends and there were often four of them, playing computer games for hours.

By the time Angela arrived at the lake, Gareth was sitting in his car waiting for her. She noticed that he had a top of the range blue BMW, with black windows. His front window was open, and his radio blasted out. Despite it being late February, the sun was warm today, but the wind was cold. Angela had put on a black dress and jewellery. She'd also spent a lot of time on her hair, which looked great. She chose a short jacket beige with a fur collar. Her appearance was both smart and sexy, and her hair bobbed in the wind.

"Hello again, I love your hair. Have you had it done?" asked Gareth.

"I did it myself. I thought I'd smarten myself up a little. A gym teacher can be glamorous," she replied, laughing a little.

"Ah you're a gym teacher, that's why you look so fit", said Gareth.

Angela smiled and didn't comment, but she'd already noticed from a distance, that Gareth smelt heavenly. She wasn't entirely sure what it was, but it drifted around the car. He quickly reversed, stopped for a second and said, "Right, you and I are going to have some fun!"

Angela suddenly felt a sense of excitement that she hadn't experienced for years. She thought about how lucky she was to be dating this gorgeous man, although she wondered what happened about the walk.

"I couldn't have the boys, this weekend after all, so I just came out to meet you. I've been busy getting some plans ready for this new restaurant. It's been hell to be honest, with people not pulling their weight, but I'm getting there now. The kids are with their mother today, but I'm worried about her. She doesn't seem to be coping with them very well. Then, there's Daisy, she seems to be causing nothing but trouble," said Gareth, who looked irritated. He also looked annoyed at the traffic which was building up, and started to frown.

"Ah, Daisy, that's your daughter?" asked Angela.

"Yes, my daughter. She's not my biological daughter, but I've always been her father. When I first met Linda, she already had Daisy, a six-year-old from a previous relationship, so I took her on. She's now seventeen, and at times, she's a nightmare. She doesn't get on with the boys because they are only ten and eight. They get on her nerves. She spends a bit of time with her real father, but he's a waste of space, so it's better in a way that he doesn't bother. It isn't good for her to have an unreliable influence in her life. He works in London and abroad. He's always busy, sorting loans and debt collecting. I really wouldn't like to get on the wrong side of him though," said Gareth, looking anxious. Angela noticed the stress appearing on his face. She thought that the traffic wasn't that bad, so why was he so uptight?

"Well, I'd imagine it's a big job to take on someone's child, but I also think it's brilliant that you have. Although, they say that teenage girls are far harder work than boys", she replied, trying to think of something appropriate to say.

"You can say that again. Right, Angela, we're nearly there now. I'll park where I usually park, and we can walk the rest of the way. Then, we'll have a bit more time because if we park closer, it's only for an hour," said Gareth, who suddenly appeared more relaxed.

"Brilliant, whatever you think best," replied Angela. She'd already noticed that she was moving too much into her dumb blonde mode. She checked herself for not having an opinion and thought she better watch this as their dates progressed! This was definitely where her relationships had failed before, by not speaking up. Perhaps she needed to enjoy it and allow herself to be taken care of for once. She knew that having been a single parent for so many years, she sometimes found it difficult to trust others to take care of her needs. She had to stop taking control or she might spoil everything.

Very soon, they were at Reds, sitting on two stools, overlooking the boats in the Marina. The sun was out, and everything looked bright and clean.

"Ah, that's better," said Gareth, taking a little sip of red wine.

Angela was surprised how closely they sat. Their knees were touching but she enjoyed Gareth's closeness. It made her excited. It was noisy in the wine bar, but they could still hear each other, without raising their voices. For some reason the weather was much warmer here than by the lake and people flooded onto the outside patio area, in the hub of the Marina. Angela leaned forward to talk to Gareth. She could feel his breath on her face. Despite a few worry lines, he had a sincere and handsome face. She hoped that her intuition was right about him and he was as genuine as he appeared.

Angela had always been intuitive but she sometimes regarded it as more of a curse than a blessing because she didn't spend enough time getting to know people. Then they'd let her down. Her assuming would stop her from asking the relevant questions. She recently realised that a lot of her past relationships had been built on illusion. What she imagined they were, rather than what they were! This time she had vowed that she'd ask anything she needed to know. She wanted to be bolder, so she knew exactly where she stood. She was already sensing Gareth had his hands full with his children and work, but the attraction between them was pulling her in. She was intrigued by his daughter, but if she pressed him for more about that, she felt sure that he'd become agitated and she wanted to keep things light today, so they could have fun. Her attraction to Gareth was a nice feeling, and it made her feel young.

"You look serious. Have you been working too hard? How about a holiday? Anything planned with your sons?" he asked.

Serious, thought Angela, if only he could read her thoughts!

"Well, I thought I might take them walking in the Lake District, but I'm not sure yet because I'm going to Turkey in May. Hopefully, Marcus will be going to University in September, so this summer will go quickly. We're waiting to hear if he's got into his first choice, but we've still got a few to visit. It's been a long and complicated process, sorting it all out. We might not know for a couple of months where he's going. Believe it or not, he wants to do sport, imagine that? He's mad, but I think he'll be good at it though because he's great with kids. He's got more patience than me. His father was like that, a patient person."

"And you left him?" asked Gareth, smirking.

"Well, it's not as simple as that, as you know", replied Angela, not wishing to take it that casually.

"Ah right, what happened to your ex-husband? Does he still live in the local area?"

"No, not now, he moved to Cambridge a few years ago. He tries to see our sons regularly, but now they have their own lives; they often don't want to bother going because seeing their friends has taken over. I don't worry about it. All is good at home, but it's very hectic with me working full time, as well as having to help them. This University thing has taken up a lot of time. I've needed to take time off work. It would have helped if his father was willing to visit a few. The school wasn't accommodating either, can you imagine that when they encourage kids to go there."

Gareth laughed a little. "Yes, I can imagine that.

Being a single parent is a full-on job. Linda's struggling and as I said, I'm not sure she's coping. One day's good, another day is bad; she's constantly on the phone asking me to help her like we're still married, even though, we've been apart for several years. Linda couldn't cope without my support, so we still speak most evenings. It's a bit of a drain, but what choice do I have? If she goes under, then it will fall on me to look after the boys and Daisy. I love Daisy. But she's hard work at times. She's been rebelling an awful lot recently. Grounding her doesn't work either because she just disappears, which is a real headache. Last weekend, she had a huge tattoo done on her upper arm, and it looks terrible. She said it was to celebrate her rebirth or something? I'm not sure that she lives in the same world as I do. Then, there's her smoking. I tried to turn a blind eye to it because what kid doesn't like a puff or two, and normally the fascination soon wears off, 'the it makes me feel big thing.' The problem is it's not just about cigarettes now, is it? It's this weed stuff, or what do they call it now, skunk. God knows what's in it? All I know is that one minute she seems pretty settled and says she loves me, and then she turns argumentative and says her Mum would have been better off without me. I've never seen her smoke weed, but these out-of-control mood swings are hard to deal with. Whatever the reason is, the bottom line is that she isn't working and I don't know if she plans on turning up for her A levels. She seems to think that hanging out with her mates, smoking, and drinking is what it's all about. The sad thing is that Daisy is an intelligent girl. She used to say that she was going to be a Lawyer and help disadvantaged people, but how can she learn law if she won't study. All she talks about now is working on the market. When I remind her about the law, she says that she never said that," said Gareth, despairingly.

Angela discreetly looked at the time and suggested that they ordered their meal. If the conversation went on like this, they'd miss having anything to eat. Fifteen minutes later, she was eating the most incredible Italian food that she'd ever tasted. Gareth also looked as if he was enjoying his meal, and his mood had lifted. He appeared familiar with the wine bar because he knew exactly what to order and it smelt delicious. Angela was relieved that the conversation had now moved onto other things. He shared her passion for sport, and he started to tell her about his interest in golf. By the time they'd finished the meal and a second drink, Gareth had engaged her completely. He no longer looked anxious, and he had started to joke with her.

"I bet you look good in your gym gear Angela! Maybe we should go out for a run together, although I haven't run for quite a few years now. It would help if I was more fit on the golf course. It would improve my play."

"Yes, that would be fun. We'll have to wait until the weather warms up a bit because I'm a coward and I don't like running until the end of March, or when the sun comes out!"

"I don't mind the weather. I'm an all weathers golfer. The only problem is that sometimes it's a difficult choice between having the boys or playing. I wish there were more hours in the week. When they're older, I'll take them with me. We've already been up to the local driving range a few times, and they love whacking the balls. They've watched me play but they soon get bored. I'm hoping that they'll eventually grow into it." he said, with a grin.

"Maybe Daisy would like to play? Surely there are as many females playing as males and it might do her good?" said Angela, a little tongue in cheek.

"Daisy has a real talent for it, on the few occasions I've taken her to the driving range, she's whacked a ball further and more accurately than the boys or I. Unfortunately, right now the only sport she's interested in is shopping. She comes home with new clothes or jewellery every weekend. She appears to have more than she can afford. I don't know why Linda lets her waste her money when she'd be better off saving for driving lessons?"

Angela smiled and then spontaneously leaned over the little table to kiss him. She didn't know why she did it. Maybe it was to cheer him up or to snap him out of talking about his daughter again. It seemed to work, and he immediately perked up and smiled at her. Angela then felt his hand resting on her leg, and their bodies naturally moved closer together. She began to ache for him. She wasn't sure if she wanted this and so soon but she couldn't help it because the attraction was strong.

"You're a very sexy woman Angela", Gareth whispered across the table. Angela realised that he was also feeling the attraction.

"I try my best," she answered with a grin, as she visualised them having sex.

"I've got to get going now. Shall I get the bill?" she said, as she realised the time and stood up.

"No, I've got it," said Gareth, springing to his feet. He took out his wallet and walked over to the bar.

"That was great!" said Angela as they headed for home in Gareth's BMW. "Thanks for taking me there. What a brilliant place with great views over the Marina. Do you mind dropping me home, because I think I'd better not be driving this afternoon, I can always pick my car up later, or I could even run there!"

"No, problem, that's very wise, and I enjoyed it too. I'd love to see you again Angela, but next weekend I'm playing golf on both days, I'm not seeing the kids, which sucks. It's pretty full-on at the moment with one thing and another. Still, I'll call you during the week, and we can fix something up for the week after, if you're around?"

"Yes, I expect so," she said, playing it cool, but she was already feeling the excitement rise inside her at the prospect of another date. It also felt a little out of control.

"Maybe we can go to the coast. It could be cold, but we can easily wrap up, perhaps Aldeburgh, or somewhere not too far? Anyway, I'll be in touch," said Gareth.

They drew up outside Angela's house, on the edge of the town. Her home was on a busy road, so he had to bump the car up onto the pavement. Gareth suddenly sprung out of the car and came around her side of the vehicle to open the door. Angela couldn't believe how chivalrous he was. She hadn't experienced this before. He then gave her a quick peck on the cheek and was gone.

Angela stood on the pavement for a few minutes. She didn't feel like rushing into the house to have the boys start on at her for being late, especially as she was without the car! She suddenly felt a little giddy, she wasn't sure if it was the wine or the effect that Gareth had on her. Something about him made her feel out of control and woozy. Perhaps it was because he was always in a rush. She wasn't sure what it was, but she knew that she could easily get carried away with this light headed feeling, especially after she'd been drinking. She wanted to relax and just go with the flow, but she was afraid to in case she forgot her own needs. She wished Gareth had given her a proper kiss, but she'd wait for that kiss because he was gorgeous and she fancied him like hell. It quickly crossed her mind that he was experiencing quite a few issues with his daughter. He'd also explained that he didn't see much of her, so if they dated, it probably wouldn't be an issue. She decided to put him to the back of her mind because right now, she needed to turn her attention to her own family. She still had a lot of her parenting to do and there was no time to get involved in his family muddles. If Gareth wined and dined her, it would be fine. Even better if they had good sex, and maybe that was all she wanted. She'd been so excited about her date; all thoughts of Martin had vanished!

Chapter 5 – Back at School

It was a busy Wednesday at school and Sally, the new Deputy Head, had started. She'd asked Angela if she could have a chat with her at lunchtime to familiarise herself with a few things. Martin would also be there, along with a few other teachers.

Angela was busy teaching P.E. in the sports hall, this morning and she'd already placed the children into small groups of five to work on a combination of stretches and squats. Following that, she'd planned a few short games of basketball. They seemed happy enough. They needed to let off some steam today because it was very wet and it was also too cold for outdoor games. Angela noticed that the time was going very slowly this morning and she was relieved when at last it was their morning break so she could grab a coffee. As Angela walked into the staff room, she noticed that Martin and Sally were already there. Martin was reading some documents to Sally, who sat next to him taking notes. They both looked up at her as she walked in and smiled.

"Hi Angela, you look tired again," said Martin, who didn't care if he embarrassed her in front of the new Deputy Head. Angela was extremely annoyed, but she decided to make light of it. Being angry at Martin in front of Sally was unprofessional, and she didn't intend to stoop to his level.

"Yes, I'm a little tired, but I'll manage. I just need a little caffeine top-up," she said, reaching for the coffee. Her voice remained calm, but she was fuming. How dare he?

"This is Sally, our New Deputy Head. I'm sure you two will get on well," he said with a smile.

Angela smiled at Sally but still avoided Martin's gaze. She already knew that she didn't want to befriend Sally. However, as she always tried to be friendly with the people she worked with, she decided to welcome her.

"Welcome to Cherryfields, Sally. I hope you'll enjoy working with us. I'm sure that Martin will welcome some much-needed help. We're a very busy school, but we do have some fun, and most of the staff get on well. We also have regular meetings to discuss our progress, along with the odd chat in the staff room. I expect Martin has told you this? Ah yes, and we sometimes meet at the local pub in the evening, from time to time," Angela added, looking at Martin.

Sally smiled at her. Angela observed that her too-tight blouse, which was unbuttoned very low, was inappropriate for working with teenage children. She also wore several gold necklaces and rings, which gave her the appearance of having money.

Sally was a petite blonde lady, with wavy hair, which was held in place with a large amount of hairspray. She wore a smart short skirt which matched the colour of her blouse and a pair of dark tights and shoes. Angela thought that her clothes were a little old fashioned and more suitable for a woman in her later years. But despite her appearance, she looked immaculate and Angela felt a pang of envy as she gazed at her neat little figure. Angela wondered how old Sally was because appearances were deceptive. She assumed she was in her mid-forties, but it was hard to tell. She noticed Martin standing very close to her while he showed her the new rotas, and he leaned in even closer to point out what they needed to discuss at lunchtime.

"Unfortunately, we're going to have to rotate the teachers a little. We always have staff shortages in the winter, and temporary teachers are like gold dust, so we have no choice. We're never sent them until we're climbing up the walls. What I'd like you to do Sally, is to keep an eye on the absences and see if you can move people around to accommodate the school's needs. It's not an easy job, but it's an essential one," said Martin in an authoritarian manner.

Angela stood back and finished her coffee. She had to be at her next lesson in three minutes, but she couldn't help but notice that there already appeared to be sexual chemistry between Martin and Sally, which made her feel uncomfortable. She didn't know why it bothered her, but she knew that Martin had a special kind of magic with women and he attracted them quickly.

"I'll see you both at lunchtime," she muttered, as she abruptly left. She quickly closed the door behind her and glanced through the glass to see Martin leaning even further into Sally's space. His focus may well have been on the rotas, but he was also well into Sally's blouse.

What a creep. He was already sizing her up, as a replacement for me muttered Angela under her breath. For the first time, she felt a little sorry for Martin's wife, as well as her experiencing a pang of guilt when she thought about the sex they'd enjoyed. It had been good for her in one way because she'd come to realise what she didn't want. She'd also learned a lot about manipulation. No doubt Martin would keep declaring himself as available until he satisfied his needs!

"Right, what would you like to do today?" she said to a large group of children who'd been waiting in the hall for her.

"Football," they shouted eagerly.

"Football, did they want to do that again? Angela hated football because part of her regarded it as an all-male sport. She decided that she'd have to bow to pressure this time and hoped that they'd listen to her. She wasn't in the mood for shouting at a rabble, and the weather was still miserable.

"Ok then, we'll do football, but if you don't listen to me, like last time, I'll stop the game immediately, and we'll do cross country running instead. Now, can I please have five volunteers for team leaders, hands up?"

Angela tried not to show her feelings about the things she didn't enjoy, because to do her job correctly, she had to remain positive. Hopefully, it would be better this time, but she knew it was going to be a long day. When she got home tonight, she'd plan her trip to Turkey. May half-term would soon come around, and she was already a little excited. She needed to book her flight and buy some clothes, or she wouldn't be going.

Angela was looking forward to seeing Jean. She'd been there just over a year ago, but it felt like a long time now. Had that part of Turkey changed much and had Jean changed since meeting her new man? She hoped not, because she'd loved going there before and it would be a chance for her to soak up some much-needed sun and to put men to the back of her mind. Chris her ex, was happy to take Marcus and Shaun to Cornwall to see his mother which was bliss!

* * * * *

It was 7 p.m., and Angela had eaten. She was hastily shoving the dishes in the dishwasher when she heard her mobile ring, so she answered it.

"Hi Angela, it's Gareth," he said, in a friendly voice.

"Gareth, oh hi, nice to hear from you," she replied, feeling surprised and excited.

"Would you like to come over for a meal, on Saturday evening. I don't have the boys this weekend because I'm playing golf on Sunday and they're going somewhere with their mother. I may have Daisy, but she always plays on the computer. I'll probably cook for her as well. Is that ok with you? It won't be a late evening because I have to be up early the next day, to play golf.

"Yes, that sounds great," Angela found herself saying.

"Good, I'll see you at mine at around seven. I'll text directions. I'm not a brilliant cook, but I've been learning over the past few years, so I'm sure you won't be disappointed!"

"I'm sure I won't Gareth. It's very good of you to offer. I'm not much of a cook either, so I'm always grateful when people ask me to dinner," she said, laughing.

Gareth said goodbye and was gone. Angela could feel the anticipation rising in her. It all sounded fantastic, but she wasn't sure about Daisy. She hoped she'd like her and it wouldn't be too difficult. By the sound of things, the poor girl had gone through enough, with her mother being up and down. It was kind of Gareth to have her stay. In a way, it would have been good if they had some father and daughter time. Angela tried to stop her thoughts from escalating because she didn't know what their relationship was like, she only knew about the things Gareth told her. Although it was evident that he was trying to make an effort to get to know her and she felt flattered by that. Angela had already noticed the chemistry between them, and they enjoyed each other's company, so any other issues would sort themselves out.

She closed the door to the dishwasher and looked at the clock. Her reports needed to be finished before the evening was over. It was something she didn't feel like doing, so she'd have to force herself. At least focusing on her work would steady her a little. Gareth had asked her if she liked fish, which she did. He sounded like a great cook. She couldn't wait until Saturday, only Thursday and Friday to go!

Chapter 6 - Daisy

Daisy was up in her bedroom. Her mother told her that she needed to get up early tomorrow because she was going to stay with her dad. Daisy wanted to stay at home on her own this weekend, but her mother had said no. She was unhappy about this and thought her Mum was unfair to her because she was seventeen and old enough.

She'd angrily told her mum that she didn't want to go with her brothers to visit her grandparents because it was boring and spending hours in the car with them got on her nerves. She wanted to listen to her new cd and meet her mates at twelve tomorrow because they always hung out on Saturdays. Staying with her dad had completely messed up her plans. He got on her nerves because he had this irritating way of making out that he was young. He always asked her about her music and friends and what she'd been doing. He even said to her that she could call him Gareth. How sad was that? She didn't want to call him Gareth, or Dad, because he wasn't her dad. She had her dad, even if she hardly ever saw him; at least he sent her gifts through the post. She wanted to live with him, but he said it was impossible because of his job. He often said, 'maybe in the future, we'll see,' so Daisy lived in hope.

Daisy knew that Gareth had agreed to have her this weekend because her mother needed some space. She'd told him to 'fuck off' last time she saw him, and they ended up having a huge row. Daisy hadn't mentioned it to her mum, because she would have broken down in tears. She didn't want things to become worse. Why couldn't she stick up for herself? Gareth was such a bully. He'd bullied her when they lived together, and he was still rude now.

When Gareth left them, her mum quickly became depressed. Daisy found it hard to understand why, because she didn't need him, so why was she so upset? Her life was happy before her mum met Gareth. Even though she was young, she remembered her mother smiling and laughing. She never cried. They didn't live with him for very long, because he said it was chaotic, but it was him who caused the chaos. When the boys got a bit older, he rented a house nearby, but he still visited at odd times. Daisy was convinced this had made her mum worse, her not knowing whether Gareth was going to turn up or he was at some Golf Tournament! She was surprised he'd had her over so much lately, but she guessed it was because he'd agreed she couldn't be left on her own. He said that he got on better with her now that she was older, but that was a lie because all they did was argue. He irritated her when he stuck his nose into her business and wanted to talk about her boyfriends. He didn't understand her at all. Surely it was obvious she didn't fancy boys. He was wrong about everything, so why did he bother even trying? She was pleased when Gareth said it was over with her Mum because she didn't want to see him again, but sometime later, she reluctantly agreed to stay some weekends to give her Mum a break. Over the last few months, she'd become angry and fed up with being told what to do. He was treating her like a child, and if he did it again, he was going to get even more fuck offs, whether it caused an argument, or not.

Daisy put on her two favourite silver rings. She had quite a few now but getting the right size was sometimes a problem. She could always get rid of the ones that didn't fit her that well by selling them to her school friends. She loved amber and she had a couple of amber rings of different shades. She liked the green amber best but it was hard to get hold of. Gareth always asked her where she got it, but her Mum never asked. He was so nosey. She couldn't be bothered to tell him that her real Dad sent her some of the jewellery because he was always saying that her dad was a waste of space. Daisy felt as if Gareth was always watching her, noticing what she wore, or how she talked to her friends and it made her uncomfortable. He was the complete opposite of her Mum who never noticed what she bought, or wore since she'd been on tablets.

Two weeks ago, Daisy had dyed the top of her hair, purple and her mum didn't say a word about it.

Her mum and brothers often went up to north Norfolk, to see her grandparents but Daisy was only interested in going if it was hot, so she could lie on the beach. She sighed and started to pack her bag. She needed to get ready quickly because Gareth was going to pick her up in half an hour. How boring! Maybe she'd take a couple of films, although he'd probably talk through them. Gareth didn't approve of horror but she could watch them on her TV upstairs when she went to bed.

Daisy returned the jewellery she didn't want to wear to the box. She'd have to go out next Saturday to get some more from the market. She'd talk to Marie, who was stoned most of the time, so it was easy for her to slip a few rings into her pocket. She always felt her heart pounding but as she walked away, she'd give her a little wave. Marie never noticed they'd gone because Daisy bought a few now and then, to appear a good customer.

Daisy loved the thrill of taking rings. It wasn't often that she felt that kind of buzz, except for when she ripped open the parcels from her dad which were a complete surprise. She knew that stealing was bad but it was also exciting and she needed that thrill. She wasn't going to get it any other way unless she managed to get to Brighton to meet Sarah and she didn't have enough money for that yet. She was going to go, even if it meant selling all of her best jewellery. She'd work out what to tell her Mum when she had the money. She wouldn't bother saying anything to Gareth about it because she felt sure that he'd try and stop her but she planned to go for good.

Daisy walked out of the kitchen and opened the back door. The sun was shining, so she sat down on a garden seat, which overlooked a small charming back garden. Whoever made this garden knew what they were doing, she thought inhaling deeply into her lungs. If she had her last spliff now, she'd hopefully remain calm with Gareth, provided he didn't go on about her jewellery again. As far as he was concerned, she's got a lot of girlfriends who gave her presents.

Gareth had already told her on the phone, that some woman was coming to dinner tonight. Great, she hated being polite to his friends. It also meant he wouldn't let her spend so much time on the computer because she'd end up being sent off to bed early. She hoped this woman was better than the last one he dated, which lasted all of five minutes. She was probably sporty because all of them were and usually played golf. Daisy enjoyed golf and she wished he would take her with him. He assumed she wasn't interested or he used it as an excuse because he didn't want to pay for her. Her Mum used to go with him but she said he was always chatting to women, which made her feel inadequate. Her mum also liked sports but she preferred things like swimming and running. Her mother wasn't inadequate until she met Gareth, who constantly put her down, and then things changed.

Daisy stubbed out her spliff and then hid it at the

bottom of the dustbin. Her mother knew that she smoked but she was fairly sure that neither of her parents knew about the spliffs, just as well really because they'd be mad at her. She heard Gareth's car pull up at the front of the house, so she went to grab her stuff and quickly locked the back door. They always left a key in the garden shed in case someone needed it in an emergency. Daisy closed the shed door and went through the wooden gate to the car.

"Hi Daisy, how are you today?" asked Gareth, as he turned his head and smiled. "I thought we'd have pizza for lunch. I'm cooking a special dinner tonight because my friend is coming over," he continued cheerfully.

"A friend, what's that?" muttered Daisy, sarcastically. She didn't want to appear interested in Gareth's private life because then, he would go on about it and drive her mad.

"Her name's Angela; I told you that she was coming over on the phone, remember? She's a Sports Teacher at Cherryfields School, the one your friend used to go to. I've forgotten her name now."

"You mean Lucy. Teachers are boring. I have enough of them at school. I wish I didn't have to take my 'A' levels. I think I'd be better getting a job, maybe on the market, or something, anything. I hate studying. It's a waste of time when I need money."

"Well, you could do that but your mum and I would be disappointed because you are capable of getting good grades and going to university. That's if you try!"

"You mean you would be disappointed, Dad. I don't want to go to University, I've already told you that. Mum doesn't care?"

"We'll see", replied Gareth, who had decided to leave it for now rather than risk a full-scale argument. He was trying to concentrate on the traffic.

"Not, we'll see. Dad, you're beginning to hack me off now."

"Gareth," he said, smirking at her.

"Yeah right, Gareth. I've brought a few games to play, if that's ok and a couple of films. I don't want to go to bed early either, because it's Saturday and I could have gone out with my friends. I said I'd meet them in town today and we could go and look round the shops but Mum told me I had to see you."

"What do you want to look around the shops for, jewellery? I see that you are wearing some new rings that I've not seen before. What's that green one?"

"Green amber and I bought it last week. It was cheap from the market."

"Your mother gives you too much money, I'll have to have a word with her."

Daisy was glad she'd had the spliff because if not, she would have thumped him! She climbed out of the car and followed him into his modern, three-bedroom detached house. It wasn't very imaginative for an architect, but Gareth claimed that he'd bought it for an amazing price! It was an attractive corner plot with a big garden. She used to have a swing and a climbing frame, but he'd now put a trampoline where her swing had stood for her brothers. Daisy didn't mind because they usually spent hours out there having fun. It was a great trampoline, and he said that she could use it as well. It could hold an adult's weight, so there wasn't any chance of it breaking. She sometimes went on it if the weather was warm enough. It was something to do. It was too windy today. Even if her hoody was zipped up, she'd be cold, maybe tomorrow if she was bored.

Daisy had a bedroom at Gareth's but she didn't keep any personal information in their because she was worried that he might look through them. She was careful to keep her mobile out of his reach, just in case he read her text messages. There were messages from Sarah. If Gareth found out she was gay, he'd probably go mental, as he had about many difficult situations.

So, this woman was a fucking school teacher? Did he want his head testing? She probably looked good in a gym skirt or something? She wasn't looking forward to meeting her because she'd be boring. She would ask to take her dinner to her room where there was a TV and she could text her mates.

As soon as her Mum dropped her off, Daisy went upstairs to her bedroom. She'd go down later and play a few games, while Gareth was in the kitchen. She could hardly keep her eyes open and wondered if it was the spliff. It had been a strong one. Gareth sounded like he was clearing up. Later he'd be consulting a Delia Smith cookery book to find something suitable for dinner. He wasn't a great cook and he'd been through most of her recipes more than once. Daisy forgot about the pizza because she'd had a fry up for breakfast at home, so she wasn't that hungry. She was good at looking after herself and she was already a better cook than him!

Chapter 7 – The Evening

Angela was excited. She cooked her sons' pizza and chips, took a shower and put on a short plain black dress. It wasn't her most glamorous dress but it looked great with a jacket, her gold necklace and matching earrings which Chris had bought when they were on their Honeymoon, in Florence. At the time they were extremely expensive and they always looked elegant. Her short dress showed off her shapely legs. Angela stood and looked at herself in the mirror and puffed up her hair with a little gel to give it some volume. She always looked great when she dressed up. She loved looking feminine because she spent so much time in her gym gear, so wearing a dress, black tights and heels was a welcome change. As she walked out to her car, she felt a little nervous. She hoped Gareth had remembered that she didn't eat meat. She was also worried about meeting Daisy because she knew the girl wouldn't be keen to meet her. Still, she was old enough to do her own thing, so it shouldn't be a problem. She wanted some time alone with Gareth in a place where they could chill and talk together because bars and restaurants were too noisy to share anything personal.

Very soon, Angela walked up the path of a nice looking detached modern house. It was still light and she could see some primroses and daffodils in the garden. Someone did the gardening. Did Gareth have the time? If he'd did it, he'd done a great job because the borders were perfect. The bell buzzed loudly and Angela quickly stepped back from the conservative blue door! A shape appearing through the glass panel which she didn't recognise. The door opened and there stood a girl which she assumed was Daisy.

Daisy had long dark hair which was dyed purple and cut very short on the top. She wore a small nose stud and she had several ear piercings. Her fingers were laden with silver rings and she wore a long green amber necklace, which looked stunning. Angela noticed that she was an attractive girl, with huge dark piercing eyes. She was average height, around 5 ft 5 inches tall but her shoulders were slightly slumped as if to keep out the world. Daisy's jeans had a large rip over one knee and she wore an open black hoody with Linkin Park printed on the front. Angela noticed that she looked slightly annoyed and she guessed that she didn't want to answer the door.

"Come in," said Daisy, as she glanced at the floor. Angela was aware that she didn't want to make eye contact with her, so she didn't engage her in conversation.

"Thanks," said Angela as she walked into the hallway. She then noticed that Gareth was standing in the kitchen cooking. When he saw her come into the house, he walked over to greet her and took her coat.

"Ah Angela, hello, you're in good time. You've met Daisy then?" he said, giving her a brief kiss on the cheek.

"Yes, it would appear so," she replied, smiling at them both.

"I'm going upstairs," said Daisy, as she turned quickly to walk away.

"Come into the lounge Angela, I'll grab you a drink. Dinner won't be long. I've made us a veggie paella. Then, we're having cheesecake. I hope that's ok?" he said.

"Yes, that sounds fine. I've brought some wine, not that I can drink much because I'm driving," replied Angela, handing Gareth a bottle of chardonnay.

"Well, I've got a spare bedroom, if you want to stay," he said, casually. Daisy normally goes up to her room around ten and she's out like a light. I don't know how she does it. Angela just smiled at him because she had no idea at this point, whether she wanted to stay, or not, but she didn't want to get into a sexual situation with Gareth this early on.

Gareth had made a good job of the paella and the aromas that came from the kitchen were incredible. He insisted that Daisy joined them for the meal, although she'd made it obvious that she didn't want to eat with them. Gareth firmly told her that having dinner in her bedroom was rude and if she joined them, she could use the computer when they'd finished. Daisy quickly succumbed to Gareth's bribe, because she wanted to play computer games. She was surprisingly hungry, after missing lunch. She hoped that she wouldn't be asked about her A levels again because if that happened, she'd be off.

Angela thought the meal was lovely especially the paella and she complemented Gareth on his cooking skills, especially as he wasn't vegetarian. Daisy didn't say anything during the meal because she wasn't interested in anything that Gareth had to say. He talked continuously about his photography and golf which Daisy had heard many times before, so she switched off. She noticed that he didn't bother to ask Angela about her work or hobbies but she seemed happy to listen to him.

After dinner, Daisy quickly settled down on the computer in the dining room, while Angela and Gareth took their wine into the lounge to sit together on the sofa.

"What would you like to listen to?" he asked.

"I don't mind," said Angela, "surprise me."

Gareth put on some soft background music, saying it was smooth Jazz. She was impressed by his efforts and she leaned back against the sofa and sighed. The room was very comfortable and she felt relaxed. She noticed there were some great photographs on the walls which she found very interesting.

"Do you like my photographs?" he asked, as he noticed Angela looking at his pictures.

"What, you took these?" said Angela, who was genuinely surprised.

"Yes, I did. Some of them were taken in Spain and others are places in England. That one over there is of the North Yorkshire Moors in the autumn. Don't you think the purples are incredible? It's a fascinating yet bleak landscape in the winter, but in the autumn, you know why people call it God's country. I love walking in the hills. It's a pity Suffolk's so flat, although we do have one or two small gradients here!"

"Yes, I've seen a lot of England. Suffolk's a great place to live having the East Coast. I like to go to Aldeburgh for a walk on the beach and visit the famous fish and chip shop,"

"Yes, me too, it's not far from the golf course, so I've been there quite a bit. I'm sure we could combine the two things one day. Perhaps when the weather gets warmer, we could have a game of golf, followed by a visit to Aldeburgh and fish and chips!" said Gareth, enthusiastically.

"I'd like that," Angela said, "although I've never played golf, so I might be pretty useless but you can show me the basics. I've seen all those trophies in your cabinet. You must be good."

Gareth smiled, then he also leaned back to embed himself in the sofa. Angela felt him slip his arm around her shoulders and edge a little closer. At that moment, the door opened and Daisy stood in the doorway. She shouted "the thing has frozen again. Dad, please come and fix it because I'm winning and

I'll have to start this game all over again if you don't come right now."

Gareth stood up and put down his wine. He walked into the dining room with Daisy. Within moments, Angela heard raised voices.

"You've got an hour," he said. Then, I'd like you to go up.

"What, that's 9 o'clock. No, I'm not going up then!" replied Daisy sounding angry.

"You are Daisy!" said Gareth, sounding exasperated.

"No, 'fuck off'. It's your fault I couldn't see my friends this weekend and now you want me to go to bed early. No, I'm here until ten. That's what you said," answered Daisy, indignantly.

Gareth walked back to the lounge and smiled at Angela. He didn't want her to know how annoyed he was. Bloody girl, she's just like her mother, difficult. She would never do what I wanted either and now look at her. The woman's a wreck, she pops more pills than dinners. It's hardly surprising that she spends so many weekends with her parents because she can't cope with the kids. She's capable of looking after the boys with help, but not Daisy. The girl's such a handful and she's spoilt because she's given the money to buy whatever she wants. Linda gives in to her, thought Gareth, who felt worn down by it all.

"Would you like another glass of wine Angela? I thought we could watch a movie?" asked Gareth smiling, as he turned over the television channel. Gareth didn't wait for her answer and continued to pour another glass of wine. He then sat down and turned his body to face her. She suddenly felt his mouth on hers and before she had a chance to think, his tongue was eagerly exploring. Gareth's hand then stroked the back of her hair as he caressed the side of her cheek. His lips then left her mouth to slide down her neck. He began giving Angela gentle kisses and then he rested for a while in the nape of her neck. Angela thought that he was going to kiss the top of her breasts and she became aware of the fact that Daisy was still up. Her heart was pounding with anticipation and she started to sweat slightly. She felt extremely turned on and she knew that if she finished her wine, she'd succumb to his advances. She could stay the night if she wanted to because her sons were with their father tonight and they wouldn't be home until six tomorrow evening. She reminded herself that she was free to do as she pleased and she was allowed to relax and have fun. She had forgotten what passion felt like and it suddenly came flooding back to her. Her body was craving attention and she wanted to let go.

"Let's watch a film," Angela said, rather abruptly as she stood up to walk over to a shelf that contained around fifty films. She picked up one of her favourites, 'As Good as It Gets,' and hoped that Gareth was ok with it. She knew that they were just passing time until the inevitable. She was trying to contain her excitement and act cool, but it was proving to be difficult because she wanted this man far more than she had ever wanted Martin. The thought of Martin and his demands made her skin crawl.

Two months ago, she couldn't get Martin out of her head because she had wanted him so much, and now she couldn't stand the sight of him. None of it made any sense. She'd read in a book that sexual attraction was about energies, whereas lust was pure addiction. Was it possible for her to have sexual attraction and love together? She hoped so because she was looking for both. If she held back from Gareth, would she find love? Or would she be denying herself once again? She noticed that he was already absorbed in the film. How did men do that? They find it so easy to switch on and off. It was a complete mystery. He suddenly noticed that he was being observed and he turned his head and smiled.

"I've just heard Daisy go up. It's ten, so she did what she was asked. She must have been annoyed though because she didn't bother to stick her head in to say goodnight," he said appearing slightly anxious.

"It's probably because I'm here. Poor girl, it seems like she's having a bit of a tough time of it lately, not wanting to do her A levels and her mother not coping," replied Angela.

Gareth sighed. "Don't feel sorry for her Angela, because she can be a real monster. Sometimes I wonder why I have her here. It's not as if she's mine. I know it sounds cruel, but the older she becomes the more I realise how different we are. Apart from her being good at golf and that's just weird. Why would a girl of her age want to do that? She surprised everyone on the golf course. My friends said that she's a complete natural at it and I should bring her with me all the time. I would if she wasn't so bloody difficult."

Angela felt the tension rising. She'd drank too much wine to go home now and Gareth knew it. So, she smiled, reached for her glass and polished off what was left in the bottle.

Gareth moved close to her again and tenderly took her hand. Then he kissed her more passionately than before, pressing his body up against hers. Angela could feel waves of desire breaking through her body, which became harder and stronger until the sensation was impossible to stop. Gareth put his legs up on the sofa and she decided to do the same. They lay their side-by-side hugging and kissing like a pair of teenagers for what seemed like hours.

"That's nice," she finally said, sounding a little breathless.

"Angela, I know that we don't know each other that well, but I want to make love to you," he said.

'Make love?' The expression sounded so much better than the word 'fuck' which Martin used because it made her wince, but at the same time, it excited her and fed her addiction. Now, here was a man offering to make love to her, she sighed and pondered. She was worried that Daisy would come in and interrupt them and it didn't feel right for them to have sex with her in the house.

"What about Daisy, won't we disturb her?"

"No, I told you how well Daisy sleeps. I've checked on her many times but it's a waste of time because she's always crashed out." She relaxed and put her arms around Gareth's neck and stroked the back of his hair. She felt the muscles at the top of his arms. His body was hard and toned. She clung to him needing to be close.

Their lovemaking was frantic and urgent; Angela had to stop herself from calling out his name, for fear of disturbing Daisy and she bit the top of his shoulder. But Gareth cried out several times enjoying moving from passion, to a feeling of urgency and then surrender.

After their lovemaking was over, they lay side by side under a rug which Angela found at the end of the sofa. She suddenly felt embarrassed about her body and wanted to cover her breasts but Gareth removed the rug and gently kissed each of them telling her that she was beautiful. Angela didn't say a word but felt they had some special connection. Eventually, she got up and decided to get dressed in complete silence.

"I must go home," she said, at last.

"You can't go home after drinking all that wine. Stay tonight and we can make love again in the morning. As long as you leave by eight, Daisy will never know you stayed."

Angela decided to stay because she knew that Gareth was right. She had drunk too much. She held his hand and walked with him up the stairs to his bedroom which she discovered was an incredible room, complete with black satin sheets and mirrors! Perhaps in the eighties, he'd been a playboy but now times had changed, or had they?

Chapter 8 – Sunday

The sun shone through the curtains onto the bed and Angela awoke from a deep sleep. She'd been dreaming. She dreamt that she could hear a child crying but she didn't know who it was. She thought it was very disturbing. It felt as if a pair of eyes were looking down at her, which completely spooked her. She jumped out of bed quickly, suddenly realising where she was.

"Angela, come back to bed," said Gareth. He patted the other side of the bed, hoping she'd return.

"No, I can't. I promised myself that I would get up early and go for a run. I've got to get fitter because some of the children are fitter than I am and it's embarrassing," she said, rapidly putting on her clothes. Don't worry to get up because it's Sunday and Daisy might hear you," she continued heading for the door.

"Ok, we'll talk later. You wore me out last night and I'm still knackered. Please can you see yourself out? I'll text you soon." replied Gareth, as he rolled over to go back to sleep.

Angela remembered that he was going to golf, but he was too tired. You're not used to it she thought, as she noticed him sprawling over the bed. She was in half a mind to climb back in there, but they'd only start again. What she needed was discipline because without it, she was no-one. She could allow herself some fun but she certainly couldn't give up the things she was committed to.

Silver, her big grey tom cat was waiting to greet her. He began rubbing the side of his face against her leg because he wanted food. She quickly poured out his biscuits and put on the kettle. After a strong coffee, she'd be ready to run.

Angela found it hard. Her feet pounded against the pavement and she felt as if her head was going to burst. She also remembered her dream about the girl crying which she thought it was odd. The possibility that it could have been Daisy, made her uncomfortable. Surely it wasn't her, because if it was, Gareth would have got up to see if she was alright. She was concerned when he said, as Daisy became older, she didn't feel like his daughter. She wondered if Daisy felt rejected. It certainly looked as if she was forced to stay with him, whether she liked it or not. Still, it wasn't her business and there were so many things to sort out within her family. Marcus' university visits had to be finished. She wanted to make sure he was happy. She'd enjoyed last night. The meal was good, the music was great and the sex was incredible. She felt tired and happy but she knew running would be hard this morning because it wasn't a good idea to run after eating late and drinking so much wine!

Angela had run around 3km, when her body ached so much, she felt like giving up. The underneath of her feet also felt sore and her knees hurt. She'd continued to jog along the road at a slower to the local park where she ran around the perimeter, twice. She ducked her head under the same branches which needed cutting back. Although it was a lovely spring-like day, all she wanted to do was go home and rest.

Highfields Park was extremely picturesque with its many beautiful trees, shrubs and colourful flower borders. It was very busy today. There were Mums with their children on swings and families feeding the ducks at a large duck pond. Angela often ran here because it was closer than the lake. Although she still preferred the peace of the lake, especially early in the morning. That was enough for today. She could only manage three kilometers instead of five but at least she tried. Angela remembered it was important to pace herself! She eventually ran up her garden path and burst through her front door for water. If she wanted to regain her former fitness, she'd have to work harder. Maybe she needed to stop drinking wine altogether that would help. She also wanted to get fit for her holiday, which wasn't long now. But today, she had to settle down and plan her lessons for the coming week, which would take her a good couple of hours. She knew she had to take a copy of her schedule to Martin first thing on Monday, which she wasn't looking forward to. If there was a way that she could avoid him she would. The last thing she needed right now was sarcasm.

Chapter 9 – Golf

"Daisy, can you get up now please, I've got to get to golf and I told your mother I'd drop you back to the house on the way," said Gareth, giving her bedroom door another knock.

"Yeah ok, just give me a minute and I'll be up," shouted Daisy.

"No, I can't give you a minute because I'm already going to be fifteen minutes late. Please get a move on."

"Ok, ok, I'm up," said Daisy.

Gareth heard Daisy plodding around her room. Eventually, she went into the bathroom. He quickly went into her room to open the windows and immediately noticed a strange smell. For a minute, he had a flashback to his student days. He recognised that sickly sweet smell. No wonder she was knocked out for hours on end! It was weed. For a moment, he felt as if he was going to explode. Then he got hold of himself, quickly shut the door and walked into the kitchen to make a coffee. He didn't want to confront Daisy now, because he knew that it would make him late for golf. No doubt there would be tears, denial and all sorts of other emotional stuff. She'd say that he didn't care about her, which wasn't true. He had heard it so many times and he always reassured her that he did care! It wasn't his fault if she didn't believe him. Bloody girl, he needed to drop her off on time because at this rate, he could well end up watching which was a waste of time!

"Make sure the door's shut properly Daisy," shouted Gareth as he sat in the car, revving the engine. He'd hit the horn once and he felt his anger rising to an uncontrollable level.

When Daisy finally appeared, she looked as if she had been dragged through a hedge backwards! Her hair, which looked reasonably tidy yesterday, was now a mop of back and purple. Her eyes looked puffy and gave her the appearance of having very little sleep. Gareth thought the only attractive thing about his daughter were her silver rings. He still couldn't understand why she had so many. He hated the nose ring she wore. It was vile but he knew better than to ask her to take it out because he'd receive another 'fuck off'! She was entitled to a bit of individuality, as long as it didn't reflect on him. He flicked back his fringe and looked in the car mirror, making sure that none of his neighbours were watching. They knew about Daisy but he didn't want them to see her in this state. He never worried about the boys but he was quickly embarrassed by any curious looks at his rebellious daughter.

"Just drop me in town. I didn't know I was going back this morning and my mates will be there today as well. I can get a bus home later," explained Daisy.

"Yes ok, that would be better for me. Your mum

asked if I would drop you at home because they're not coming back until dinner time, but as long as you go back by mid-afternoon, that's ok," replied Gareth, smiling at her.

Daisy looked at Gareth with utter disdain. She knew that woman had stayed the night and he hardly knew her. She'd been up in the night and had heard them at it. For fuck's sake, he was so embarrassing. She hoped that he wasn't going to let her stay over again. She would give Gareth a hard time about it and hopefully he'd take her to golf and spend some money on her. It was about time he did something for her because he was always spoiling the boys. But she didn't want to go there again unless she was forced to, because she preferred playing computer games at home with her mates. Next time, she'd persuade her mum to let her stay at home on her own, then, she wouldn't have to see Gareth or that woman again. Daisy hadn't liked any of his girlfriends. They were all stupid and to easily impressed. He normally went for unintelligent women, but this one was a teacher? Still, she had nice earrings. Was too risky to try and take them? She wouldn't miss them for a few days, and by that time they'd be sold to one of her friends. She'd saved quite a lot of money and in another couple of months, there would be enough for Brighton. She couldn't stand it any longer. She'd have to get away soon. She was old enough to work and have a room somewhere. Her friends on social media said that they'd give her somewhere to stay until she was sorted. Anything was better than living here. Suffolk was the most boring place in the world. Her parents were a pain and she didn't like either of them. Her dad was a bully and her mother was pathetic and it was all Gareth's fault!

Chapter 10 – Angela

Angela breezed into school. Nothing was going to upset her today because despite her meeting with Martin, she still felt elated from her evening with Gareth. She was proud that she'd managed a short run on, Sunday. She was also looking forward to seeing Gareth again and hoped it would be soon. He said that he'd text her when she left and she was sure he would. The priority was talking to her ex about her holiday. She felt bombarded by everything and her head was full. She needed to stop thinking about Gareth and clear her head.

Angela took a deep breath, knocked on Martin's office door and went in.

"Come and sit down. I've been going through some changes with Sally. They'll hopefully make everything work much more efficiently particularly when we have less staff due to sickness. It does mean that some of your lesson times are changing. I hope you don't mind but we've had to amalgamate two of your smaller groups into one," said Martin, with a serious face. He looked a little nervous as he spoke.

Angela noticed that Sally was sitting very close to him, their legs were practically touching. He saw she was looking at them, so he stood up and walked to his filing cabinet, to take out a set of papers for her. He then decided to include Sally and as he passed a set of papers over to her, he leaned over her to achieve a better view of her cleavage. Angela found the act completely unnecessary because he could easily have passed her a copy without leering. She suddenly felt embarrassed and she wanted to leave. What was this, a display of Martin's sexuality, or a meeting about her work? It annoyed her.

"Yes, he said, suddenly clearing his throat",

"Yes what?" asked Angela.

"It's looking better now," said Martin, looking slightly embarrassed as he realised that Angela was on to him.

"It doesn't look so good from my angle but I see what you mean, I kind of expected this," said Angela, with a straight face. She decided to leave the room as quickly as possible. As she rose from her chair, she noticed that Sally, who looked slightly flushed, also stood up to leave.

"Will you excuse me," Sally said. "I think that you and Martin can sort this out between you. I need to get some water, the menopause," she said, under her breath, as she abruptly left the room.

When the door was shut, Angela gave Sally a few minutes to walk away, before she spoke to Martin.

"The menopause, yeah right!", Angela said, sarcastically. "I know it's none of my business Martin, but surely you haven't started on her already?"

"Yes, you're right Angela. It's none of your business. Can you work with these new lesson plans or not, because if you can't, we'll need to review it," he said, sounding very annoyed?

"Do I have a choice?" she asked, still feeling angry with him. A pulse started to beat in her face, her lungs felt tight and she was about to explode. Why did he always have this horrible effect on her? It wasn't as if she wanted him because she was attracted to Gareth, but he had this annoying way of pulling her back. Was she jealous of Sally? She didn't want to believe she was, but for a few moments all she could think about was the fantastic sex they'd had together and he was now giving the same to Sally. Perhaps even an improved version of him. She couldn't help but feel annoyed.

"You're jealous, aren't you?" asked Martin, laughing a little.

"No, of course not, don't be ridiculous! What would I be jealous of? It's not as if you're ever going to leave your wife, are you? You're just playing games and it's a game I'm no longer playing."

"You've still got the cutest arse in the school," said Martin, grinning.

"I'm going because you're despicable! If you must know, I've met someone and things are going well," she said.

"Well, I hope he knows what turns you on because most men don't," he replied, giving her a little smile!

Angela headed for the door. What an arrogant sod. She wished in her heart that she'd never set eyes on him. Martin often had these little jibes at her. He enjoyed pushing her buttons to near exploding point. Unfortunately, she wasn't sure whether to slap or jump on him. It was quite frankly horrible, but at the same time, she realised that she was still buying into horrible, which was worrying.

Angela walked along the corridor and opened her office door to sit at her desk. She would have to run every day now. She had no choice. If she didn't apply more discipline to her life, she could easily slip back into vulnerability. She'd worked too hard now to let Martin back. She didn't need men like him. After all, she now had Gareth, or did she?

Chapter 11 – Unbelievable

Angela was at home. She was pleased to be around for Marcus and Shaun but she decided to take herself off into the spare bedroom to start working on the end of Easter term reports. Angela looked at her huge pile of work and she was wondering where to start when she suddenly received a text from Martin. What on earth does he want she thought, as she opened his message?

'Angela, I need to talk to you. Is there any chance that you can pop out to meet me for a drink tonight?'

She thought for a few moments. She wasn't sure why he'd want to meet her and she had so much work to do that it was impossible. Surely, he realised her workload because he'd asked her to meet this deadline. She thought it was ironic that she'd not heard a thing from Gareth, but she'd heard from the man she didn't want to talk to. She quickly replied, 'Sorry, I can't meet you tonight because I've got to finish the reports.' She knew that Martin would understand this because he had an equal amount of work to get through, so she carried on with her writing. She was then about to turn her phone off when she suddenly received a second text from him.

'Angela, my life's a mess. I've had a huge row with my wife and fallen out with Sally, I could lose everything. You were right, I've been stupid and you're the only friend I've got. Please try and come. I miss you.'

Angela drew in her breath. What had happened between him and his wife? Perhaps she'd found out about Sally? Or maybe she'd got it wrong and they were just friends. She was prone to making assumptions but the fact remained, she needed to get the reports finished, so whatever it was it would have to wait. She was worried though because he sounded desperate, but didn't Martin always sound desperate? That was how he manipulated her. To say she was his only friend was rubbish because he had plenty of friends. Even if he'd got himself into trouble, he could turn to his family for help. She wasn't going to do the same as she'd always done and run straight to him. She needed to stand her ground because her life was as important as his.

Angela put the phone down and started to write the first report. Her head ached and she felt uneasy inside. She found it hard to focus which made her feel a little annoyed. She felt guilty about not meeting Martin and decided to send another text.

'Hi Martin, of course I'm your friend and I do care, but I can't meet you tonight because I need to finish the reports. I'm also picking up the boys from Basketball Club at nine-thirty, so I'm sorry it's impossible. I can do tomorrow evening though, so let me know ASAP.' She went back to her work but she found it difficult to concentrate and constantly glanced at her mobile every half an hour to check for messages. She was worried but she'd offered to meet him tomorrow. She didn't want to meet him but felt a sense of duty because they had been good friends.

Her work was finally finished so she went to pick up her sons. They had started to play computer games together, so she quickly ran a bath. They'd carry on playing for hours. It wasn't good for them, but they'd finished their work and they needed some time to relax. They'd both been working very hard studying for their exams and she was proud of them.

Angela turned the hot tap off with her foot and stretched back in the bath. She thought it was amazing how easily she did this and it meant that she could stay in the same position for ages, without getting cold. She shouted goodnight to Marcus and Shaun telling them not to go on past twelve because it was a weekday. "We know," they replied in unison, because they'd heard her say it so many times before!

Half an hour later, Angela glanced at her mobile again to see if Martin had replied, but there was still no text. She wondered about sending a follow-up message to ask if he was alright, but decided to leave it. Tomorrow would come around quickly and she'd see him in the morning.

It was Friday tomorrow and nearly a whole week had passed since she'd seen Gareth and he hadn't been in touch. She reminded herself that he said he'd text, so she needed to be patient. She was annoyed at herself for sleeping with him so quickly. Perhaps he'd used her. Was he seeing other women as well? Daisy wasn't at all impressed when she was introduced to her, maybe she was fed up with meeting dad's women and she was another one? Angela noticed that the same old feelings of disappointment began to surface. Why did she always feel like this? She wanted love and she deserved it. Every cell in her body craved it so why did it constantly escape her? She wondered whether to send Gareth a nudge by sending a text. It was coming back, this feeling of being out of control and slightly obsessive. The last thing she wanted to do was to transfer the sexual obsession she'd experienced with Martin onto Gareth.

Angela laid the towel on the end of her bed and looked at her naked body in her full-length mirror. She knew that she was attractive and had a good figure. What was wrong with these men? She needed her holiday. Perhaps when she returned from Turkey things will make more sense. She didn't want to be serious with anyone until she knew them and she didn't know much about Gareth. Angela suddenly felt very sleepy, so she climbed into bed to read her book. Five minutes later she was sound asleep. Her mobile began ringing at 5 a.m. She thought it was her alarm so she chose to ignore it. It was way too early in the morning to react. When the sound went on and on, she finally answered the call.

"Yeah, who's that," she managed to squeak out?"

"Hello Angela, It's Sally from Cherryfields. I'm sorry to trouble you this early, but something terrible has happened. Martin was very strange last night and we had a bit of a row. After that he didn't speak to me all evening and when I tried to get in touch with him late last night, there was no reply. I'm so sorry, this is awful, but I've just had a phone call from the Police to say that Martin was found dead in the boys' toilets in the early hours of this morning. The caretaker found him."

Angela didn't understand why Sally was phoning her, or why Martin was in the toilets in the early hours of the morning? She was still half asleep. What was Sally saying?

"What do you mean in the boys' toilets?" she asked, trying to wake up so she could take it in.

"I mean that Martin hung himself with a piece of rope, from a pipe in the boy's toilets," said Sally as she became uncomfortably louder.

Angela went cold. She felt sick. She thought about the text messages she'd received from him last night, and she quickly grabbed her phone to read them. If only she'd gone to meet him, she might have been able to help. This couldn't be true because Martin would never do something like that. He had a few odd ways but this wasn't like him at all.

"I'll get dressed and come in," she said. She didn't know what else to say. Martin had wanted to discuss something but she had no idea it was so serious. Had she realised, she would have left the reports and met him. She felt terrible. She shakily threw on an old pair of jeans. She didn't care what she looked like when she needed to get to the school as quickly as possible to find out what was happening. She needed to speak to Sally about last night, preferably before the police spoke to her.

When Angela arrived, the police were already all over the school. They'd put tape across the entrance to the boy's toilets to cordon off the area. Fortunately, Martin's body was no longer there but Sally was there and she was a quivering wreck.

"I'm so sorry, Sally, I'm shocked. Martin contacted me last night because he wanted to tell me about something but I said I couldn't meet up with him until today. He also said that he'd argued with you?" Angela continued keeping her voice low so that only Sally could hear.

"Yes, I had a huge row with him. He said he was going to leave his wife and move in with me. I told him that he couldn't because I wasn't ready. He said that he had to because his wife had thrown him out and he had nowhere else to go. When I still refused, he said that for now, he was going to stay with a mate but we'd talk about it in the morning. When I told him no, he was really angry and completely flipped out. He said that I owed him because he made me Deputy Head over another good candidate so I owed him a favour," explained Sally through her tears.

Angela felt sick. She was in extreme shock. She felt a lot of compassion for Sally but at the same time, she was relieved that Martin hadn't asked to move in with her. Perhaps that was his plan? He'd been rejected, so his next step was to persuade her and she was the mate.

Angela wanted to go back to bed and pretend this nightmare wasn't happening. She also wanted to tell Shaun and Marcus about what happened before they found out some other way.

"If you don't need me to do anything, I'll go home now. I'll be back around nine when my sons have gone to school because they'll be really worried if I'm not there for breakfast. I left them a note, but I'd better go back and explain what's happened."

"Ok then Angela, but please don't be too long because the Police want to talk to us both. They also want access to Martin's desk. They're treating it as suicide and they have an idea why he did it but they want to investigate everything thoroughly and talk to each member of staff. I've closed the school today and we're contacting the parents, which is an enormous job."

Angela thought Sally still looked shaky. She was worried about leaving her but she needed to go home.

"That's a good plan Sally but please make some time to sit down and grab yourself a coffee because you look like you need it. I'll be back as soon as I can. Please don't blame yourself for what happened because Martin was a strange man at times. I'm sure that he had a lot of secrets. I wanted to warn you about him weeks ago but he wouldn't let me near you, so it was difficult," explained Angela, who was trying to be strong.

Five minutes later, Angela shot out of the school. As soon as she got into her car, tears rolled down her face. She couldn't believe it. She needed to steady herself so she could face her boys. Neither of them knew that she'd been personally involved with Martin. They'd both gone to Cherryfields and they knew that he was the head. She'd told them that she met Martin for meetings but that was all.

Angela was relieved to be home. She pulled into her driveway and noticed a Magpie sitting on the lawn. As she walked up to the front door it just stood there hardly moving. She turned to face it and said, "You know don't you, you spooky bird. Why are you following me? I should have taken more notice of you when I saw you tapping on the window. Now it really is one for sorrow." The Magpie flew into next door's tree and she quickly wiped away her tears.

Angela closed her front door. She always felt safe in her home because it was a comforting place to return to. It had a healing energy which often made her want to stay at home. Marcus and Shaun were still in bed, so she put the kettle on to make a cup of tea, before giving them a call.

She finally arrived back at the school at 9 am. Marcus and Shaun had been shocked by the news but they were very grown-up about it. Angela felt that she was talking to two very understanding adults. They said that Martin could have been depressed, or had other problems. She decided that she'd never let her sons know about their short relationship because they didn't need to know and now there was little point.

As soon as Angela walked into the school, Sally hurried towards her with a look of panic on her face.

"Oh Angela, thank goodness you're here. The police want to talk to you now. They also want the key to Martin's desk. I can't find it anywhere so maybe he hid it somewhere? I have no idea why he would hide it but we have looked amongst the other keys and it's missing. The one that's meant to fit his desk doesn't fit. It's very strange. Perhaps he changed the lock?"

Angela thought for a moment, she remembered what Martin did with the key. When they were together, he'd taken a blanket out of his desk drawer and put it in a strange place. She was going to ask him about it but she didn't want to spoil the moment.

"It's under the plant pot, on the window sill," she told Sally, and with that, Sally rushed off to find the Police Inspector.

Angela went up to the staff room and helped herself to a very strong coffee. She was still in shock and it was going to be hard to hold back her tears. She needed to calm down and think about what she was going to say to the Police. Their friendship was obvious but she hoped that it wasn't necessary to talk about their affair. Perhaps his wife already knew what had been going on? Or, maybe she knew about Sally. She had asked him to leave, so she must have known something but how much? That was the question!

Angela breathed deeply trying to bring in her mindfulness. She needed to prepare for what lay ahead. Before she'd finished there was a sudden knock on the door and in walked Sally with the Police Inspector.

"Hello, I'm Police Inspector Stephen Clarke. The good thing is that we've managed to open Martin's desk, using the key from under the plant pot, but we've found some photographs of you and some of the children. The pictures of you were taken while you were teaching games on the playing field. Martin had a lot of photographic equipment in his desk which we think he used regularly. He took some close-ups of you and the children. It would appear that he had some sort of an obsession with you. Some of the photographs of the children look as if they were taken while in his office. Although, as yet, we're not entirely sure where some of them were taken. It could have been on the school premises, or somewhere else. I'm not going to show you them because I think that you'll find them upsetting. However, because we discovered that he sent you several texts and you sent some to Martin, we'll need to ask you about your relationship with him. His wife is aware of the photographs because she'd found some at home. She'd already called the Police to report her findings before all this happened and we'd already started to investigate it."

Angela sat back down on the chair and reached for the remainder of her coffee. Her hands were trembling and she still felt sick. She had no idea that Martin had been spying on her during her gym lessons. Even more upsetting, was the fact, that he'd photographed some of the children. How that came about, she had no idea. Maybe he befriended them? Angela immediately ran to the toilet to vomit. She felt as if she was bringing up all the contents of her stomach from the day they met. Every coffee they'd drank together and the meals that he'd treated her to. Even the times she'd cooked for him at home! They were all coming out of her body as stress and total disbelief. When she'd finished vomiting, she looked in the mirror. She was white as a sheet. She'd have to go back home because she needed to get away from this school. It was like a curse and she hated it. She felt so angry at herself. Why, oh why, had she got involved with Martin? Now, the Police were going to dig into her personal life. She didn't need this. If Gareth discovered she'd been involved with a perverted head teacher, their relationship would be over. It wasn't her fault but it was extremely messy and worse, if her sons found out about their affair, she wouldn't be able to handle it.

Sally suddenly came over to her as if she was sensing how she was feeling and put an arm around her shoulders. She was still crying and deeply distressed herself, so Angela thought that she was very compassionate. She no doubt regrets her involvement with Martin as much as I do, thought Angela, as she tried to pull herself together.

"Look, take all the time you need ladies. We do

appreciate that it's an awful lot to take in right now. We have to return to the station to carry on with our investigations and possibly work with a specialist team. We will come and see you both again if we have any more questions, but for now, I suggest that you both take a few days off to rest," said the inspector.

"Thank you for your time," Sally mumbled, as he walked out of the staff room. She then turned to Angela and said "the school will have to stay closed for a few days, or possibly a week because of the boys' toilets and then there is the press to worry about. I don't want to close but we'll re-open as soon as things have died down a little."

Angela was still thinking about Sally's thank you to the Police Inspector. That was a joke. Thanks for what? For turning their world upside down, or for the realisation that she'd been involved with a possible paedophile. She knew that the Police were only trying to help, but it didn't help and it put the school in a terrible light. Still, just because Martin took a few pictures, didn't mean that he was one, did it? He could have just had some weird obsession with looking at pictures of the children. There didn't have to be anything sexual taking place but even that, disgusted her. She'd done it again hadn't she? She had to stop making excuses. When would she ever learn, and what about Martin's obsession with her, that was unnerving? She'd been stalked and it felt horrible. 'Admit it Angela, however kind you are about Martin, he had some serious issues going on," she said under her breath. She felt so tired all she wanted to do was sleep for the rest of the day. The police still had to interview her, but she'd deal with that when the time came. If she played it down a little and said they went out for a few meals together to discuss work, it would appear quite innocent. They hadn't seen each other for a few months so it wasn't relevant? What was more important was Sally's relationship with him and the row the night before he committed suicide because he could have revealed to her what was going on? But the bigger concern was definitely the photographs of the children. She found it hard to believe that he would do such a thing and now the school had no Head Teacher. That was a problem. Fortunately, Sally was going to sort things out in the interim. It would be good for her to run the school until they found someone permanent because it would help take her mind off things. It must have hit her badly.

Angela quickly left the school, got in her car and headed home. As she was nearing home, she heard her mobile ring so she pulled over to see who was calling her. To her surprise, it was Gareth. She decided not to answer him because she needed to switch off her phone and rest. She didn't want to tell him about Martin because she wasn't in the right place. How could she have been so deluded. It had shocked her.

* * * * * *

Fortunately, both Marcus and Shaun were out when Angela arrived home. She rested until the evening and watched the news. She always found it depressing, so she quickly turned it off and listened to music instead. Then, she remembered about Gareth's missed call. Was it too late to give him a ring at nine-thirty pm? Well, it was before ten, so he'd probably still be up. She felt butterflies in her stomach as she called his number. She put it down to nerves because she was keen to speak to him. At least he'd be a distraction from what had taken place earlier.

"Hello Gareth, it's Angela. I'm sorry to call you so late but I've had a hell of a day, and I've only just had a free moment. How are you?" she asked enthusiastically.

"I'm great, thank you. I'm pleased you rang because I wanted to see if you'd like to pop over on Friday evening. We could catch a film or something? Is there anything special that you'd like to see? I haven't been to see a film for months but I'm told there are several good ones out."

"Well, I can certainly find out," she replied. Maybe if I come to you, we could go for a quick drink, then make the late showing," she suggested.

"That sounds great to me. If you come here around seven, we can take it from there?" he replied, sounding positive.

"I'll see you then. I won't talk now because it's late and I've been feeling a little under the weather all day. Still, I'm sure that I'll be fine by Friday."

"Under the weather, well that's an old-fashioned saying but I know what you mean. Perhaps we could roll like thunder under the covers again," he replied.

"I guess that's why they call it the blues," replied Angela laughing. Gareth had a way of perking her up which made her smile.

"See you soon, then," she replied. His joke was a little corny but she was still excited by him. She laughed to herself and decided to put the television back on. She very soon became immersed in a new detective series which was good. After half an hour or so, she couldn't keep her eyes open and fell to sleep. Her sons returned from their evening out to find her crashed out on the sofa, snoring!

Chapter 12 – Friday Evening

Angela found it a rush. First cooking for Marcus and Shaun then clearing up to be ready to go out in the evening. She quickly slipped on a pair of black jeans, with a long-sleeved tee-shirt which glittered with sequins. She pulled down her top to reveal a bit of cleavage because she wanted Gareth to be attracted to her. At the same time, she didn't want to make it too obvious that she was attracted to him, by being too revealing. Angela had a good figure and her jeans clung neatly to her buttocks giving her the appearance of a much younger woman. She'd styled her hair then scrunched it, so it easily fell into place, which gave her a trendy look. She wore light makeup with bright lipstick and she'd painted her nails. She liked her appearance tonight, despite the mad rush and she was excited about seeing Gareth. She quickly slipped on her coat so that her sons wouldn't make any comments and shot out of the door. She knew that there was an air of sexuality about her which was inappropriate for them, so she shouted goodbye and left the house. Half an hour later, Angela pressed Gareth's doorbell and quickly stepped back to wait. She was surprised when she saw Daisy come to the door, to greet her.

"Hello Daisy, I've come over to see Gareth. Is he here?"

"Dad said, if you arrived before he got home, I had to ask you in. He's not back from work yet."

"Not back from work? Well, that's ok; I don't expect he'll be long." It was obvious to her that Daisy wasn't going to say much. She walked into the house and decided to sit on the sofa and watch television until Gareth returned from work. Something important must have happened to hold him up because he hadn't said anything about being late when they spoke on the telephone.

"Do you want a coffee or something?" asked Daisy.

"Yes, please Daisy. White no sugar," Angela replied.

A few moments later, Daisy walked into the lounge with two cups of coffee. She put her coffee down on the table and passed Angela a cup.

"I'm going to finish my game. Here's the TV remote if you want to put it on. Dad's always late home from work. He probably got a later train or something. If he misses the early one, he'll be here at half eight," she said, as she walked into the dining room.

Half eight, that meant that she'd have to wait an hour for him, after all that rushing around. She felt agitated but she knew that it was hardly Gareth's fault, if he'd missed the train. It was Friday evening and he had to get right across London. She thought for a minute, then felt annoyed because she was at it again, making excuses for men.

There were several good programs on Friday evenings and before long she was lost in one. She leaned her head back on the sofa cushions and started to drift off. She was sound asleep when the telephone started ringing. For a few moments, Angela wondered where she was. Then Daisy stomped into the lounge to answer the phone. She looked really angry at leaving her computer game.

"No, I'm afraid Club isn't here. He's out and no, I don't take messages for him," said Daisy, slamming down the receiver.

"I'm not his bloody messenger," she said angrily. As she spun around to walk away, her hoody slipped off one shoulder and Angela noticed that she had some huge bruises on her upper arm.

"What Club?" Angela asked, trying to get Daisy's attention.

"Club, oh, that's my dad. Though he isn't my dad he's Gareth. I hate calling him that too. He gets called Club by other members of the Golf Club. They think it's a joke but it's not a fucking joke, they're sick. He used to threaten to hit mum with his golf club and I know he did. When they split up, she tried to tell some people about it and he said she was making it up. No-one believed her, which made things even worse for us. He told people at the Golf Club that she'd made up a story and they thought it was a huge joke. They didn't reckon that anyone would do anything like that. Especially not Gareth, their golden boy. He's won all those trophies in that cabinet over there. That's why he got the nickname, Club."

Angela was horrified. She stood still for a moment, not knowing what to say. She didn't want to believe Daisy, although she looked like she was telling the truth. She looked very scared and the story was bizarre. It sounded like something out of a Bond movie. Still, why would Daisy make it up?

Daisy quickly pulled her hood back up over her shoulder and zipped up her hoody.

"Please don't tell Dad what I said, or he'll make my life hell. It's bad enough as it is," said Daisy, looking anxious. She looked Angela in the eyes, then sat down on the edge of the sofa to light a spliff.

Angela looked at the spliff and decided that she'd turn a blind eye to it. She didn't care. It was up to her and under the circumstances who could blame her. She looked at the clock, it was now eight fifteen and Daisy had said Gareth would be home around eight-thirty, by the time he drove home from the railway station. Angela wasn't sure whether Daisy could accept affection, but she decided to walk over and hug her. She completely froze and looked uncomfortable. Angela moved a little further away and gently took her hand. It was obvious that she was trying to hold back the tears and didn't know how to handle things.

"I'm sorry about your dad, Daisy. I don't want to stick my nose in your business but those are big bruises on your arm? Did he do that to you?"

Daisy completely ignored her and turned away. "I want to finish my game now. Dad will be home soon and I don't want to talk about it," she muttered while walking out of the room.

Angela knew that Daisy was scared of telling the truth, but if Gareth had hit her mother, then, it was possible that he also hit Daisy. She quickly looked at the time, he'd be back at any moment and if she left now, it would look suspicious and he might guess that Daisy had said something to her. She had to stay and pretend that everything was fine. They could go straight out to see the film because there was no longer time for a drink. She'd decided that however well they got on this evening; there was no way she was staying the night. Not over her dead body.

A few minutes later, Angela heard the front door open and Gareth quickly walked in, put his briefcase on the table and walked over to her.

"Hi Angela, I'm so sorry I'm this late, please forgive me. I missed the train I planned to get by three minutes, so I had to get the late one, which was packed. I've had something to eat already. I'll go and have a quick wash and shave and I'll be with you in five minutes. We'll still catch the start of the film. Thanks for waiting for me. I hope Daisy looked after you?"

"Yes, she's been great. She made me a coffee and showed me where you keep your remote," said Angela, as she smiled at Gareth. She wanted to appear as normal as possible.

Gareth smiled back and quickly dashed upstairs. Angela noticed his golf clubs were sitting in the corner of the room. They reminded her of the horrific story Daisy shared with her earlier and she felt very uncomfortable. She took a long deep breath and touched up her makeup. She then quickly pulled up her top because the last thing she wanted to do now was to encourage him. She'd decided that this evening was going to be their last date, but how could Daisy handle him on her own? The girl needed support.

Half an hour later, they walked into the cinema and purchased two tickets to see the Two Lovers, which Angela thought ironic. Gareth said that a friend of his had seen the film and it was exceptionally good. The storyline was not as straight forward as it sounded and the acting was brilliant. Angela liked romantic dramas, they were her favourite and she began to relax. She wanted to forget about what was said earlier in the evening. She stretched back in her seat and dipped into a small bag of popcorn that she'd brought with her. There was no way that she was going to pay cinema prices when she could go to a shop.

Gareth turned his phone on to silent and put it in his pocket. He lent across and whispered, "see, we made it in good time. We haven't even finished watching the commercials yet, so there was no rush."

Angela smiled and said nothing. Her mind was still going over Daisy and Club. She wanted to get to the bottom of why Daisy had large bruises on her upper left arm but she knew that none of this was going to be easy. She was frightened of Gareth and she didn't want to make him angry.

Gareth suddenly took her hand, and holding it firmly on his lap he said, "We should have sat in the back row, so I could put my hand down your top like a couple of naughty teenagers." he whispered. Pure romance, thought Angela, feeling a little annoyed. She hoped the film would be worth it. The film was good, and it finished at eleven thirty. They then drove back to Gareth's house. Angela wished that she could drive straight home because she was tired and it was raining. She felt like snuggling down in her bed, pulling her duvet over her head and forgetting about the world. She didn't want to think about Martin, Gareth, or Daisy. All she wanted to do was sleep. Tomorrow, she'd get those clothes for her holiday. She needed a new bikini and towels for the beach. She was short of summer clothes and it was going to be very warm in Turkey. Jean had told her to bring as many clothes as possible because she didn't want to be washing. She was leaving at the end of next week and the time would go very quickly. Her mind drifted off and she didn't speak to Gareth.

"You're very quiet Angela. Is anything wrong?" he asked as they approached his home.

"Yes, I'm fine thanks. I've just been thinking about what to take on holiday. I leave at the end of next week so I'll have to finish my shopping. The boys are excited about going to stay with their dad. He's taking them away, so that's one thing I don't have to worry about," she said, keeping things light. She was careful not to lead him into an intimate conversation because she wanted to get away as quickly as she could.

"You deserve a break. You work so hard. You'd better watch out for those Turkish men though, you'll have to fend them off," he said, grinning.

Angela was still deciding how to fend Gareth off. Should she phone the Police now and say she was worried about his behaviour towards his daughter? It was very difficult because she hadn't known him long and how did she know if Daisy was telling the truth? She smoked weed, so what if she didn't pay for it and made someone angry. It was possible that someone else gave her the bruises, although she sounded genuine. There were many ways it could have happened but it was still really worrying.

"We're here at last," said Gareth, as he quickly got out of the car.

Angela also got out, then hastily walked towards her car, feeling thankful that they'd got back relatively quickly.

"Angela, don't just walk off, shouted Gareth. What on earth's the matter with you? Aren't you coming in? I thought that..." his voice trailed off as he started to walk towards her.

"Gareth, I'm sorry. I don't mean to be rude but I have to go home now. I had a text from Marcus to say that he's ill and could I come home and that was over an hour ago!"

"I didn't hear your phone go," replied Gareth, sounding annoyed.

"That's because it was on silent, while we were

watching the film. Don't you believe me?" Angela said, hoping that he'd swallow her excuse.

"Of course. I believe you Angela, but I'm disappointed because I was looking forward to us having a really good fuck tonight."

Angela stood there for a few moments. She didn't have a reply. It was obvious to her that Gareth wasn't the romantic man she thought he was. Had he said that? He was turning out to be an entirely different person from the one she'd met at the lake. He sounded more like Martin.

"Come here, at least let me kiss you before you go. I was only joking," he said.

Angela walked towards him and gave him a small kiss on the lips. She didn't let it linger. As she pulled away, he took her hand. Where are your rings?" he asked.

My rings? She wondered, as she looked down at her fingers in the moonlight. She must have taken them off when she was washing up the coffee cups, earlier in the evening. They must still be in his kitchen.

"I'll go and get them for you," Gareth said, as he hurriedly walked to the house.

"There are three of them and they're near the sink," Angela shouted after him.

She didn't follow him, fearing if she did, he'd persuade her to stay. He quickly returned with the rings and handed them to her.

"Thank God for that. For a moment, I thought Magpie might have taken them," he said, smiling.

"Magpie, who on earth is that?"

"Oh, that's Daisy's nickname. She's got a hoard of silver rings and other bits of jewellery, so I call her Magpie. I tease her about it but she'll never disclose her treasures. She just loves collecting things. That reminds me, I've got to speak to her Mum about her spending because it's getting out of control. She ought to be saving up for driving lessons, not frittering her money away!" mumbled Gareth, as he finally walked away.

Angela felt relieved he'd gone and she started her car. Three for a girl, she pondered and smiled. She couldn't ignore what Daisy told her and she wouldn't abandon the girl, however difficult it proved to be. It must have been Daisy sobbing on the night she stayed. It was beginning to make sense now. But for the time being, she had no choice but to remain friends with Gareth, until she discovered what was lying at the bottom of this nest. One thing was for sure. It certainly wasn't pleasant.

Chapter 13 – Back to Work

Angela arrived at school with her schedule for the week ahead. She decided to discuss any changes, with Sally but it looked fairly straight forward which was a positive thing. After having a couple of days off, she needed to get back to work or she'd fall behind, even though part of her still wanted to rest at home for a few more days. As she walked into the school, Sally hurriedly approached her.

"Angela, the Police have been in touch with me and they want to talk to you today, at the Police Station. I had to go there while you were away and I must warn you, that they're not afraid to ask personal questions!"

Angela looked at Sally. She looked as if she needed support because she looked very tired. She decided that it was time for them to have an honest talk, to clear the air.

"Let's go up to the staff room to talk. If that's alright with you?" asked Angela. "We should have had this chat a long time ago. It will be good to be more open with each other about everything, especially concerning Martin."

"Yes, let's talk. I agree that it will clear things up between us and I want to ask you about a few things which have been bothering me," replied Sally, feeling relieved at Angela's suggestion.

It was early and they were lucky that they had the whole of the staffroom to themselves. Angela poured them both a coffee and they sat down in two comfortable chairs.

"Angela, I know this is difficult, but were you involved with Martin?" asked Sally, before she had a chance to open her mouth. Angela was alarmed by her directness but she decided that she may as well tell Sally the truth because it would be easier for them both in the long run.

"Well, we went out on a few dates, nothing serious. I didn't want to carry on the relationship because I knew he was married. Even though he was unhappy at home, I didn't want to be the other woman, so I finished it a few months before you started here," she said, trying to make light of it.

"So then, he went on to me. From the moment I set foot in Cherryfields, I was aware that Martins' eyes were on me. At times it made me feel uncomfortable but at the same time, I felt flattered that he took such an interest in me. Within a few weeks, he was pressing me to go out on dates with him and I didn't want to do that. I enjoyed the flattery because I haven't been in a relationship for a long time, but I wasn't interested in his demands. I had a feeling that he'd been involved with you, but I wasn't sure. He acted very strangely when you were around, almost rude. I knew that he was trying to hide something. One day I went to his office at lunchtime and the door was closed. I noticed that he always ate his sandwiches while you were taking gym lessons. I tried the door handle but it was locked, so I knocked on the door. He came eventually but it was obvious that he didn't want to open the door. Through the gap, I spotted he had a camera on his desk and a plastic sandwich box. I told him that I had to alter some of the lesson times and I needed to talk to him straight away, but he wasn't interested. He tried to block the door with his body so that I couldn't see inside but I'd already seen some things on his desk. I wanted to ask what he was doing but I was afraid because I'd only been working at Cherryfields for a couple of weeks and I didn't want to risk losing my job. I also didn't want to get involved in something that was none of my business. I reluctantly agreed to meet up with him on a friendship basis from time to time and we quickly became very close," explained Sally, who was crying.

"Please don't blame yourself, Sally because neither of us knew what Martin was capable of. The night before his suicide, he messaged me to say that he'd had fallen out with you, that's why he wanted to meet me. Neither of us could guess what happened between him and his wife. I think she probably threw him out after discovering the photographs. I don't know if she knew about my relationship with him. I hope not, because it would add insult to injury. I'll pop down to the Police Station this afternoon and give them a statement. I don't understand about any of this photography stuff. It has shocked me. It makes me uneasy to think that he was taking pictures of me. I was being stalked and that's a complete invasion of privacy. I'm off to Turkey at the end of this week and I'm sure that by the time I get back, a lot of this will have blown over, however upsetting it is. The press will soon lose interest. I feel sorry for the children because it's not good for them to have a Head Teacher who committed suicide. What a bad example. It will make them feel dreadful when they use the toilets," Angela said, taking a long deep breath. She felt as if she'd talked long enough.

Sally walked with her to the door. She gave her a quick hug and said, "Thanks for explaining things to me. I know how difficult this must be for you and how upset you are. Don't worry coming back this afternoon because you might be there longer than you think. We have your class sorted out, so if it gets late, just go home and put your feet up."

"Yes, I will," replied Angela. Anything that took her away from Cherryfields was a bonus because all she wanted to do right now was to pack and leave for Turkey.

* * * * * *

It was two-thirty pm and Angela parked her car at the Police Station. It didn't take long to get there because it was only a few miles from the school. Her head drove her crazy as she tried to work out how much of the affair she'd reveal to the Police. She didn't want her business spread all over the newspapers, so she had to be careful. For one, Shaun and Marcus would find out and two, it could ruin her reputation as a teacher. There was also her relationship with Gareth, the least he knew about this the better. If he found out her relationship would be over and it would be impossible for her to help Daisy. She wasn't going to think about that situation now, because the most important thing at this moment was her own family.

Angela was very soon sitting on a rather uncomfortable chair, in front of two Police Officers. She breathed in deeply, trying her best to keep calm. Her stomach was full of butterflies and she wished that she didn't have to go through this on her own. Both of the officers told her their names, which Angela immediately forgot. She just wanted to get it over and done with! After this was over, she'd head into town to get her holiday shopping. Hopefully it would be over quickly, she thought, anxiously.

"So, Angela, am I right in thinking that you and Martin were close? We found your mobile number on his phone and we have a copy of the communication between you both for the last three months. We also understand that he asked you to meet him for a drink the night before he committed suicide," said the female Police Inspector, a blonde chubby woman wearing casual clothes. She smiled at Angela which changed her appearance from intimidating to human. Angela relaxed slightly, took another deep breath and then decided to go for it.

"We worked together, so Martin would have my telephone number. We sometimes met to talk about things that happened at the school. Such as parents' evenings, or staff meetings and general problems. We needed to communicate frequently," she answered, as convincingly as she could!

"Were you friends?' the woman continued.

"He thought we were friends," said Angela, decisively.

"But you didn't?"

"To be honest, I didn't like Martin that much. He was always asking me to meet up with him. I knew that he was married, so I didn't want to get involved with him," said Angela, hoping that this would satisfy their curiosity. It would also give them an explanation as to why he was stalking her, without explaining about the affair.

"But you did meet up with him, didn't you Angela, on numerous occasions and from your texts, it would appear that you were in a relationship with him."

The police officers both looked at her intently, but she decided it would be wise not to comment.

"I'm sorry to inform you that we've found some photographs of you naked, on Martin's office desk. We found several hidden cameras in his office, not just the one he used to film you with the children, but a few others. We also think he may have lured children to his office to take pictures, after school. We haven't fully investigated this yet, but it doesn't look good."

Angela felt sick. This interview was proving to be far worse than she imagined. What on earth must they think of her compromising herself with Martin in his office? There was no sense in denying the relationship now.

"Oh my God," she said, not caring what they thought of her blaspheming. She then said it several more times and continued to mutter under her breath. She also began to shake and tears rolled uncontrollably down her face. The second Police Inspector handed her a tissue and then sat back in her chair. She waited for a few minutes for her to compose herself before she carried on.

"Look, we understand that you and Martin were close at one time and we know that he was still pursuing you. If it is any consolation, we also found some similar pictures of Sally. The man was a sexual predator and we're not judging either of you. Our only concern is that you and Sally tell us everything that you know about Martin and his behaviour, so we can find out what went on. We need to get an idea if this is part of a larger problem, such as a paedophile ring," she said.

The second Police Officer appeared to be making notes and she just let the blonde woman lead the investigation, apart from the occasional smile. Angela felt that the smiles had turned from re-assuring to sarcastic and she just wanted to go, anywhere, just escape.

"I had no idea about the photographs," said

Angela, in complete disbelief. The thought of Martin's behaviour made her skin crawl. What a pervert. His poor wife. She must be devastated by everything. She probably had no idea what was going on.

"It would be kinder if Martin's wife didn't find out about the affairs," said Angela, hoping they'd agree.

"We don't intend making our discoveries about you, or the new acting head, public. To be honest your pictures aren't relevant to our investigation. We're more concerned about the children but we do recommend that you don't say anything about this to anyone. We want you to make a statement today, but we can leave it at that."

Angela felt extremely relieved and started her statement by answering the Police's questions with absolute honesty. She felt very stupid about trying to hide the details of her affair because she now realised that it wouldn't do her any favours. She had woken up to the seriousness of the situation and honesty was the only way forward. When they finally finished the interview, she thanked the Inspectors and to her relief, she was shown out of the door.

It was now 3.45 pm and Angela stepped into the car park. The sun was out and it was warm. It wasn't worth returning to Cherryfields this late in the afternoon, so she drove into town to get her shopping. She needed this holiday now and thankfully it was only a few days away. The first thing she was going to do when she got into town was to have a large cup of tea and cake.

Chapter 14 – Turkey

Through the plane window, Angela viewed a vast expanse of clouds below that extended as far as her eyes could see. She found the experience uplifting and although she didn't normally like heights, surprisingly, she felt safe. She wished that she could walk along the wing of the plane and lie in the beautiful clouds so they could act as a healing blanket. Her very own silver lining.

Angela was pleased to be taking some space from Gareth. She'd told him that she'd see him on her return but was vague about when. He appeared surprised by her casual approach. She knew he liked to be in control and she thought it would challenge him. She wanted to take charge of her life and who knows if she did, he might even miss her. It felt as if she was already giving away her power by telling herself lies. How could she know how Gareth felt about her when she didn't know him well enough yet. There was an initial connection between them but it didn't feel like love. Since Daisy explained about his violent nature, she couldn't bear him being close, so why would she want him to miss her? It didn't make sense. Part of her wanted to hold onto the fantasy that said he was a nice guy and her mind kept changing the script from reality to fantasy. She wanted to believe he was more than he was. She realised that this could be dangerous because if she believed Gareth was a nice guy, she'd put both herself and Daisy in danger. She didn't know why she did this but she needed to change her thoughts and stop excusing his behaviour. She turned on her mindfulness CD and was relieved that she'd brought it with her. The more she practised being mindful, the more aware she became, which made it easier to dump the old script. The story that no longer served her.

Angela hoped that her time with Jean would give her back the strength she needed. She still felt battle-scarred from Martin and she didn't want any more. It was even more difficult when she was at school because Sally never stopped talking about him. How she missed him, or how she was incapable of doing his job. One half of her felt empathy towards her, and the other half of her felt like giving her a shake because she needed to wake up. It drove her mad knowing how unaware she was when the truth was staring her in the face. Martin had been a user and abuser who'd only cared about Martin! Whatever attraction Sally had for him was lust, not love. How could she have fallen for him in just a few months? But it was easy to remember what it was like to be vulnerable and with Sally being a divorcee, she understood. After all, she had succumbed to his charms. He appeared to have something that other men didn't. Angela had to admit that at the time, she'd been fascinated and excited by him.

The plane continued to climb, and as it did, Angela's ears popped. The blue of the Mediterranean was beneath her. It wouldn't be long now until they landed at Dalaman airport. She leant back and shut her eyes. It felt like a very long time since she'd seen Jean. They'd been such great friends at Loughborough University, studying together and sharing student halls. How quickly their lives had changed.

Jean met a man shortly after she'd left University, and she quickly settled down. For many years she'd worked part-time as a teacher at a school in Leicester. She divorced about five or so years ago because her husband suddenly declared that he had a relationship with a man. Jean always thought there was a problem with their sex life, but she had no idea that Philip was gay. It was a harrowing time for her, but now her children were in their twenties and independent her life had picked up. She was now free to do as she pleased, so she decided to move out to Turkey. During the last five years Jean travelled all over Turkey to many different holiday destinations. She felt it was her spiritual home. While she was visiting Istanbul, she bumped into an old university friend called Jack. They'd both liked each other years ago and they were amazed that their paths had crossed again. After many meetings and long conversations, they started dating seriously. Angela knew a lot about this relationship because

Jean had always kept her up to date with her romantic life. They emailed and chatted on the phone regularly. Sadly, Jean's relationship with Jack didn't last long, but they remained great friends. Jean said that Jack was still very single and he hadn't met anyone serious since their relationship ended.

Jean then lived on her own for about a year until out of the blue, she met a young Turkish man called Alp who owned a very successful bar-restaurant. In recent months she also started working there, and she loved it. Jean was still interested in sports in general but preferred working in a more social setting and with adults, rather than children. She occasionally did a little basketball coaching to keep fit. Jean loved her villa and the Turkish lifestyle. She was thrilled that she'd now met a man who adored her and it was a bonus that he was also gorgeous. They weren't planning on getting married yet, because of the age gap. She wanted her children to be comfortable with it first, and she thought that they needed time to accept him. Jean often told Angela that she felt twenty so how could it be wrong? She had the lifestyle she wanted, the romance, the sex, the social interaction and the home. She'd received a generous settlement from her husband five years ago, which she'd invested. It had enabled her to purchase her first apartment in Marmaris. She was also an accomplished local artist selling her paintings of the harbour to local gift shops. Because of this, she was frequently regarded as a local and she was well accepted in the community.

Angela was convinced that Jean would never want to return to England and she secretly hoped that she'd find the same love for Turkey as her friend. Whatever happened this week, she was determined to relax and have fun. She wanted to be open to new experiences to take her mind off the chaos at home.

The plane finally landed and to Angela's relief, it was an easy landing. She was so eager to meet Jean that, she couldn't wait to leave the plane. She hated the boring part where she had to wait for the people in front of her to get off first and she started to feel impatient. She carried two small hand luggage bags with her, so she didn't have to go to the bag collection. It made things a whole lot easier and saved time but she still was impatient in airports because there were just too many queues.

Angela confidently strode across the forecourt and joined the next queue of people who were entering the small airport. A wave of heat suddenly struck her, it was now 25 degrees and it wasn't even lunchtime. If it got hotter this afternoon, she'd roast. While she waited, she quickly applied her suntan lotion so she didn't burn. The passport checks were fast, although Angela thought the officials looked intimidating. She quickly walked through the gate and saw that Jean was waiting for her. At least she thought it was Jean because she looked like an entirely different woman. Jean walked towards her and grabbed hold of her for a long awaited, hug.

"Angela, wow, it's so good to see you. It's been far

too long. Come over here and meet Alp," she said, smiling.

"Hello, Alp, pleased to meet you. Have I come to the right country, perhaps I should have stopped in Switzerland," she joked, giving Jean a little nudge?

"The same bad jokes then! I know that we're going to have great fun together, especially when we start on the raki. Just like old times," said Jean, giving her a wink.

Angela noticed Alp grin. She wasn't sure whether he'd grasped their conversation because Jean had told her his English wasn't good but he appeared to understand the important words!

"You look great Jean and so different. I can't believe it. The sun and sand suit you. You've got a great tan and you look so young," said Angela, feeling slightly envious.

"Sun, sand and sex. It all helps to keep me youthful. We've had such great weather here for this time of year. It's good weather most of the time, apart from when we have flash floods in the winter. It's been really hot for the last few days and it's continuing all week. So, we're lucky! Give Alp your bags and he'll put them in the boot. Look, I've still got my old number plate," replied Jean, pointing.

Angela read the number plate, 'JS10VIT' and she laughed.

"I remember that number plate, you had it on your old mini, the one you used to have at university. It cost you an arm and a leg at the time but it was money well spent because it works!"

"Yes, and I do just love it. It does work because I love my life here. The more I love things, the more I find things and people to love," said Jean, slipping an arm around Alp to squeeze him.

"Thank you, Alp," said Angela, as he shut the boot. "I think I need to be more positive Jean. Then, I can attract someone who thinks I'm beautiful and loves me for who I am."

"You are beautiful Angela. The problem is that you never see it. We'll look out for a number plate for you, perhaps one that reminds you of that fact. Now, we've got to get back and eat because it's nearly lunch time and I'm hungry," she said, as Alp started the car. "Wait until we take to the hills. You ain't seen nothing yet until you've been over the mountains. I hope you brought your hiking boots so we can do some walking together, just like the old days. It's over an hour's trip to Marmaris and you're going to enjoy the ride, so hold onto your hat."

"What hat?" Angela said, laughing a little.

"No sun hat, you're going to fry. Just make sure that you put your seat belt on because the Turks aren't the most considerate drivers and we don't want to fall off the side of a mountain, do we? I always let Alp drive because he's used to it," said Jean.

Angela quickly belted up. Jean's humour had made her feel better already. At last, she had the opportunity to let her hair down and she smiled. She then started to laugh. It was a little random, but she couldn't help it because she could feel the excitement rising within her.

"What! Are you laughing, already?" asked Jean.

"Yes, because I was just thinking about the old times when we raced everywhere to get into all those bars before closing time. We were always chatted up," said Angela.

"The good old days, eh Ang. One thing's for sure, you'll be chatted up left right and centre here, along with a few offers of marriage. It's flattering but don't say yes too quickly, because it'll land you in a whole load of trouble. Just look at me, I keep saying no to Alp and he keeps on asking." she said smiling. "I just love it."

Angela didn't think she was in danger of anyone proposing to her, so it wasn't a problem but she was happy for Jean, so she smiled and then looked out of the car window. The journey from the airport to Marmaris was proving to be very interesting with some stunning scenery. They passed some small but charming Turkish houses. Some of them looked in a little sad. There were also goats everywhere and she was fascinated by their ability to climb straight up the side of mountains.

As they approached Marmaris, the scenery rapidly changed from traditional houses to newly built apartments and villas. Money had clearly been invested in tourism and it became obvious to Angela that the more rural areas also needed some investment. Tourism had spoilt some of the charm, which was a shame. She wondered how much of the old Turkey remained? She would ask Jean later because she'd travelled extensively.

Thankfully, they'd only had a few close shaves along the journey, with sharp bends and sheer drops where Angela was forced to close her eyes. Alp had shouted in Turkish at several drivers along the way, but after the hazards had gone, he calmly carried on as if nothing had even happened. He appeared to be an amazing guy.

Chapter 15 – Arriving in Marmaris

Approximately an hour and a half later, they finally arrived at Jean's villa. It took longer than she expected because they had stopped to admire the incredible mountain views. Angela hoped that she would overcome her fear of heights as the week went on because the scenery was stunning and she wanted to see everything.

As they approached the Villa, Angela was amazed. It was far bigger than Jean's previous property. There were four large bedrooms, a good size lounge with an adjoining dining area, plus a huge kitchen. All of the floors were tiled with what appeared to be local stone. Three of the bedrooms had ensuites. There was also a small room that was used for storage, which Jean said could accommodate a single guest. Throughout the villa were brightly coloured drapes hanging from the walls, with flamboyant Turkish rugs which lay over the stone floors. In the living room there were two large comfortable sofas, with a wood burner in the corner of the room. The ceilings were high and although all on one level, the villa had a very spacious feel. Beyond the kitchen was a small outside area with an ornate patio. There were various trees and shrubs which created a relaxing place to sit. Angela noticed a brightly coloured hammock under a tree which she knew she'd want to rest in during her stay. What a dream she thought, bliss. There was plenty of space for a large family or a group of friends to stay and feel comfortable.

Angela could hear the sea and realised that the harbour was a stone's throw away. She could smell the sea air and breathed in deeply to take it in. The surrounding mountains were breath-taking and people were paragliding. Beyond the patio she noticed a small swimming pool which was shared with the adjoining apartments. Angela couldn't wait to get changed and go for a swim because she was so hot after her long journey but she was happy to wait. They were going to have lunch soon because they were all hungry.

"Jean, this place is fantastic. How on earth did you find it?" asked Angela excitedly.

"Well, Jack helped me to find this one. Although, as you know, this is the second villa I've lived in and it's definitely the best. Jack now lives in a similar one, just around the corner when he's not on his yacht. Honestly Angela, it was a real bargain. If I tell you how much I paid for it, you wouldn't believe me. I know that the prices of villas like mine have gone up recently. At first, I felt a little sad that it didn't have its own pool, but it's only shared with six other properties. I never see anyone in there and it's maintained by a management company so they keep it clean for us. We can swim later because I think you may need a little rest right now; you look dead beat. Alp and I always have a siesta this time so we'll be up in about an hour. Would you like me to show you your room?" asked Jean. Angela was hoping that they'd have lunch first, but she was happy to wait and have a short rest. The journey and the heat had taken it out of them.

"Yes, that will be brilliant, thanks Jean", she said.

Jean showed Angela to her room which was the second-largest bedroom. She was astounded by how clean it was. She didn't know how she had time to do everything, especially as she worked in the restaurant. Angela noticed that she'd gone to a lot of trouble to make her room fresh, with white bed covers, cushions and toiletries ready for her use. There was even a dressing gown for her and some brand-new slippers.

Angela thanked Jean for all her help and laid back on the bed, sinking her head into the squidgy pillows. A magazine had been left on the bedside table and she started to flick through it. This was a dream. She was going to have a fabulous week and for once she was able to relax. She noticed a couple of Jean's paintings of the harbour. They were charming and it was obvious that Jean was a talented artist. Angela felt a mixture of fatigue and excitement as she laid the magazine back down on the table and she soon forgot about being hungry.

Jean suddenly knocked on her door and then

opened it slightly. "Angela, take a rest for half an hour, then we'll have lunch. Later we can go for a walk around the harbour, you'll find it interesting. I'll show you where I sit and paint. I've asked Jack around for dinner tonight, so we'll be a foursome. I don't ask him often, with him being my ex, because I don't want to stir things up with Alp. Not that Alp would be annoyed about anything. Jack and I are the best of friends and our relationship was a long time ago now. He's on his own, like you. I think you'll like him. It's strange that you can't remember him from our university days, because he was there. I think you met him briefly last time you were here. Anyway, we'll see you in a while," said Jean cheerfully closing the door.

Angela was very tired. She closed her eyes and thought about the car trip and the crazy mountain bends. Her heart was completely in her mouth when they swerved out of the way of one Turkish driver. But Alp was laid back about it. Nothing seemed to faze him. He seems a friendly, chilled out and gorgeous looking guy, thought Angela feeling slightly envious. He may be thirteen years younger, but somehow, they looked right together. Maybe it's because Jean looks years younger than she did a year ago. Her skimpy shorts, figure hugging tops and fashionable sun glasses suit her. She may have looked strained before because she was getting over Jack. She remembered that Jean was gutted by their breakup, but she knew that he wasn't right for her. Jean had told her that Jack wasn't the settling down type and she felt that he couldn't give her the love she deserved. He was too much of an adventurer and he'd be better with a woman who was able to just drop everything and do what he wanted. Angela did remember briefly meeting him in a restaurant but it wasn't a good time for her friend and nothing much was said. She thought that he was very attractive with a huge amount of magnetism which she'd always found a fatal combination!

* * * * *

An hour later. Angela awoke to an extremely hot room. The sun was streaming through the binds onto her face which had made her come around quickly. For a moment she wondered where on earth she was. Then, she remembered her holiday in Turkey. Ah yes, she thought, as she quickly became orientated. The villa was very quiet and apart from the gentle sound of distant waves, she couldn't hear anything at all. She decided to take a quick shower and dress in some more appropriate clothes, and then she'd see what Jean and Alp were up to. Her shower was amazing and she felt refreshed, so she got dressed and opened the door to tiptoe out in case they were still sleeping. As she left her room, she heard noises coming from the bedroom. She decided that rather than embarrass her hosts, she'd return to her room for a short time, to read her book. As she turned around, she heard Alp say "You know

I love you, Jean. You're such a beautiful woman. I want to marry you, soon."

Angela couldn't hear the answer to Alp's words, but she was amazed by what he said. How do these Mediterranean men do romance so well, when all she'd experienced in the last year was a perverted head teacher and a man who bullied his wife and daughter? Maybe she should change her number plate now because she had to do something, however crazy it seemed. Jean could be right; it might help her attract someone who thought she was beautiful. It was working for her friend!

Angela tiptoed back towards her room, trying not to disturb the loving couple. She wanted to giggle at how ludicrous it was imagining her life would alter because of a number plate. She also felt like a naughty schoolgirl, sneaking back to her bedroom before anyone heard her. Jean must have stirred because she suddenly shouted.

"Angela, we'll be there in a minute. We're still having a siesta. It's so hot. Lunch is ready, so please help yourself. It's all laid out in the kitchen. We'll join you shortly and then we'll go for that walk."

* * * * *

The harbour proved to be as beautiful as depicted in Jean's paintings and the Turkish people were polite and friendly. Although Angela only knew about three words of Turkish, she tried her best to say thank you.

Half an hour later, Angela, Jean and Alp sat in a little cafe overlooking the sea. They were having a few cold drinks to cool off because the temperature seemed to be rising by the minute. She noticed that the cafe sold drinks similar to cafes in England but the Turkish brands were cheaper. This was great if she was able to remember the names.

Angela looked at Jean's outstretched legs which were a beautiful golden brown. Hopefully, it wouldn't be long before she also got a tan especially in this heat. She suddenly felt the sweat pouring off her and asked if they could move to a table in the shade. Jean continued to chat about her paintings, which she'd begun to sell in many of the gift shops, and she planned on making a website.

"You're very talented, Jean", said Angela.

"Thank you, I work hard at it. I don't do it for money, although that comes in handy. It's just so relaxing and it makes me sit down and keep still, especially after some long shifts at the bar," she said, smiling.

Jean's phone bleeped and she realised that she'd received a text. "Ah, he's on his way. Not bad timing for Jack. He's usually late."

"What, he's coming now? I didn't think he was coming until tonight?" replied Angela, wishing she'd fixed her hair and makeup.

"Yes, he's on his way. I wasn't sure if he would come today because he's been working, but it's great he can make it. I think you two will get on really well.

Did I tell you, that Jack used to work in Istanbul and he now lives in a villa, only five minutes away? He doesn't work much now. Well, he buys and sells holiday apartments and works mainly online. We always joke with him about how lazy he is. When we come back after a long shift, he's doing his work next to our pool waiting for us! I have a shift Tuesday evening but I'm sure that you'll be fine with Jack, or doing your own thing? Here he is," she said, enthusiastically then gave Angela a little smile.

Angela turned her head and noticed a tall blonde man heading towards them. Jack wore a white short-sleeved shirt, which was half open with a pair of shorts, which came just above his knees. He had a lovely physique and good muscular legs which were well tanned. As he came forward to greet them, he stretched out his arm to take Angela's hand.

"Merhaba", he said, smiling at her. She repeated the same back to him then reluctantly let go of his firm hand hold. Jack then pulled up a nearby chair to sit next to her.

"Angela, ah yes, I remember you. Not from the UK because I don't think we met there, although I was also at Loughborough. I think we met briefly when you stayed with Jean last year. How's life been treating you then? I hope that you can cope with this Turkish weather because it's very hot here. I love it. I sail around this fantastic coastline and also explore some of the Greek Islands. This place is a dream."

"You go that far? Jean told me that you had a yacht. I don't think you had that when I was here before?"

"No, probably not, I've had it for six months now. My property business is doing well and I've started to reap the rewards. It's so different from teaching sport. I did a lot of sailing in the UK. It's always been a huge passion of mine, but it's now my life. If you are staying for a few days, you can come with me on one of my trips. I'm going out tomorrow afternoon if you want to leave the love birds to it?" he asked, grinning.

Angela noticed that Jack and Alp appeared to be great friends and she couldn't sense any animosity between them. Alp smiled at Jack and once again, Angela wasn't entirely sure if he understood everything that was said. Perhaps this was useful to Jack!

"Has anything exciting been happening in the UK?" asked Jack suddenly. "Jean said something about your head of school committing suicide? That's bloody awful. I hope that you've got someone good to replace him. Poor sod. What was he like? He must have had some real problems to do something like that," he continued, completely catching Angela off guard.

Angela was shocked. She had no idea that Jack knew anything about her work and she realised that Jean must have told him. She wondered for a few moments whether it was appropriate to talk about it, but as he knew half the story it couldn't hurt.

"Martin was a good friend of mine, as well as being an excellent head. He'd had a row with his wife and she threw him out the day before it happened. The shocking thing was, the Police found some pictures in the drawer of his office desk and they suspect he may have been involved in a paedophile ring. His poor wife found out the hard way when she discovered some pictures. That's probably why she kicked him out and who could blame her?" Angela explained.

"Christ, that's bad. I bet that upset everyone big time. The teachers, kids, everyone. What about the Deputy Head? Is the school open now?" asked Jack, appearing quite concerned.

"Well, that's Sally and she's fairly new. She's been doing a great job but she's quite emotional. It's difficult for everyone at the moment because we're all still in shock. We simply had no idea about the pictures and what's even more horrible is, the police found some pictures of me. Martin was stalking me, well kind of stalking me. He took pictures of me in my gym gear," explained Angela, realising that she didn't want to go into detail. She'd come to Turkey to forget about Cherryfields.

"Really, well, I can't blame him for that, but seriously that's awful. I hope that the Police get to the bottom of it soon. Not that it helps his poor wife, she must be gutted."

"Yes, now you understand why I need this holiday," explained Angela.

"Yes, I can imagine. You'll feel different when you leave here because Marmaris is a fantastic place to chill and it has some great bars. The harbour just does something to you. You'll see a traditional way of life that's often forgotten. It slows you down and the sea, well, have you been in it?" asked Jack

"No, I haven't had a chance yet, because I've just arrived."

"Jean says we're going to have dinner soon but after that we'll go for a late-night swim. We can also try out a few bars."

"Do you think I'll keep awake that long?" replied Angela, laughing.

"Yeah, course you will, you'll be the life and soul of the party," he said, smiling.

* * * * *

The sea was as Jack described, absolutely incredible. It was midnight and the water was deep indigo but despite it being night time, it was still beautifully warm. It looked like a huge warm bath, illuminated by the moon.

Angela floated on her back and gently wiggled her toes. All the stress from the last few weeks seeped from her body and was carried away by the gentle waves. She soon began to feel lighter, almost childlike. She was discovering something new, total freedom. She began to feel that she could live her life any way she wanted and she was embracing a new start.

Jack came towards her and they swam together, splashing, laughing and racing each other. He was a very good swimmer and Angela couldn't keep up with him. "That's my yacht over there, would you like to come and have breakfast with me in the morning?" he asked.

"Which yacht? I can't see it but why not, that sounds great. I won't be up that early though because I'm on holiday."

"I'll meet you at the end of that Jetty over there at 9 am. No need to rush because I never eat that early and after breakfast we can plan our trip," said Jack enthusiastically.

"Plan our trip? That sounds interesting. Shall I wear my sailing outfit", she said, laughing.

"Just bring a bikini," and with that Jack kept on swimming until he became a speck in the distance. Angela then decided it must be time for bed.

Chapter 16 – Heaven

Angela woke early the next morning. She thought she was in heaven. She remembered her amazing evening in the company of three fabulous friends. They had started with a great home-cooked Turkish meal, with plenty of local wine, they then danced their socks off, followed by an incredible midnight swim. How lucky Jean was to live in this gorgeous environment where everyone seemed so relaxed and friendly. She had giggled with Jean about old times and Jack had poked a bit of friendly fun at her.

"That's it", Angela told them, "I'm so tired now I have to go to bed!"

It was at this point when she was just walking to her room, that Jack followed and persuaded her to go for the midnight swim!

Their breakfast was amazing. There was fresh yoghurt, nuts and honey, gorgeous local bread, beautiful fresh fruit and coffee. Yes, plenty of freshly ground coffee, which was what Angela needed. She rested her bare feet on the wooden deck and felt the warmth of the sun as it shined down on Jack's stunning yacht. Wow, it was beautiful and she felt extremely lucky to be sitting here eating this amazing breakfast with such a lovely man.

"Alright?" asked Jack. "It's nice to see you looking so relaxed, catching a bit of sun. It's surprising how hot the sun is even at this time in the morning?"

"Yes, the deck is very warm. What a beautiful boat she is, so smooth and elegant."

"Yes, she's lovely. She's not my dream yacht but she can't half move gracefully. You'll see her in action later. That's if you'd like a little sail. We can go out for a short trip, maybe later this afternoon? Please relax now and enjoy your breakfast. It's great to have your company.

"Do you miss the UK?" she asked, as she struggled to find something interesting to say.

"No, that part of my life is over. I'm so busy now selling holiday apartments, there's simply no time to think about it. I plan on doing this for another five years or so, while people interested in the area and then I'll probably quit and put my feet up by the pool. I'll leave some time for sailing of course. I've been considering teaching holidaymakers some basic sailing skills when I have the time. What about you Angela. Are you happy?"

"Am I happy living in Suffolk?"

"Ah, Suffolk, so that's where you live. I used to have an aunt who lived in Aldeburgh but I haven't been there for years. It's a great County though, having both the coast to visit and the beautiful countryside!"

"Yes, everyone says that, she pondered, remembering her conversation with Gareth. I love my job. Well, I did, but things have become difficult since Martin went and to be honest it's become a bit of a strain. Fortunately, it won't be long until both my sons are at university. I'm hoping to hear about Marcus being accepted somewhere, any day now. I still can't believe that he chose to do sport. He doesn't want to go to Loughborough, Birmingham is his first choice, but he may well be offered a place at more than one. He's always been bright," said Angela, with a note of pride in her voice.

"Have you anyone special in your life?" asked Jack, suddenly changing the subject.

Angela was quite taken aback by this question because he'd asked her out of the blue. Did she have anyone special? She'd thought Gareth was special, but she'd got that wrong. Her thoughts immediately drifted back to Daisy. She didn't want to see Gareth again, but she wasn't going to abandon the girl. But then again, she wasn't her responsibility. She took a swig of coffee while pondering Jack's question.

"Well?" Jack, asked patiently.

"No, I haven't got anyone special," she answered decisively.

"The men in Suffolk must be mad. Are they still running around in loincloths and throwing women around?"

"No, don't be daft, we're not that primitive. We paint our houses pink and a lot of them still have straw roofs but ..."

"So, can I be the big bad wolf and huff and puff until your house is blown down? Then, I can whisk you off on my yacht to sail to the far ends of the earth," he whispered, moving close.

It was an odd conversation for a man she'd just met but he made her laugh. She knew Jack was only pulling her leg and she liked it.

She finished her fruit and pushed her chair back a little to sit in the sun.

"Wow, it's so beautiful here. The harbour, beach and the mountains. There's everything anyone could need!"

"You wait until we swim in the crystal-clear bay this afternoon. I can guarantee you that you will never experience anything like it. It's incredible," he said, eagerly.

Angela couldn't help but feel enchanted by this man. He was gorgeous, intelligent and funny. He was also pressing the right buttons, but more importantly, he was here right now and they were in a place where they could relax. Life had suddenly become easy!

"Let's go and meet the others," she said decisively. Jack grabbed her hand. I'll help you get onto the jetty because it's a bit tricky." he said guiding her towards the edge of the boat. Jack quickly leapt on it first and stretched his arm out to help her. She put her hand in his and he said "jump." It was only a tiny jump but as she jumped, she naturally fell into his arms. His sincere face was smiling at her. For Angela this was something she'd never experienced. His face had nothing to hide, no smirk, mask or I told you so, nothing but sincerity.

"Thank you", she said, as she walked ahead of him. Angela was still smiling from their encounter, when she suddenly felt a tap on her shoulder. For a moment her heart stopped. The tap was identical to the one she'd received down by the lake, from Gareth. Why did it feel like the same tap? Was there something here she needed to learn? It was very strange.

"You forgot something," he said, as he passed her handbag.

"Thank you, yes I did," she whispered as she leant forward to give him a small kiss. As she did so, a spark of electricity hit her lips which made her jump back in shock but Jack just grinned.

"Electric lips. I like that," he said, and they carried on laughing.

Chapter 17 – Virtuous

The four friends were on the deck of Virtuous enjoying the sun. Angela thought she was going alone with Jack, but Jean decided they'd escort her on her first trip, because they still had some catching up!

Jack stood at the wheel, whilst Alp chatted to him. Angela and Jean were seated at the side of the deck. They leant over to see right to the bottom of the clear blue water. The wind had just picked up and although it was still warm, there was a marked difference in temperature from breakfast this morning and the water was a little choppy.

"If we see everything, we want to then we'll be very late back, tonight," said Angela. She felt excited because she was looking forward to seeing some more of the amazing coastline and exploring sacred sites. There is so much to fit in and not that much time, she thought, wishing she could stay longer.

"Oh, don't worry about that Angela, we're sleeping on the boat tonight. There are some fantastic restaurants here, so I don't think we'll want to leave early." Jack answered, smiling.

Angela wore a bright green bikini, sunglasses and

a light jumper which was tied around her shoulders. She needed to keep warm and she wished that she'd brought more clothes with her. She applied more suntan lotion to her legs which were turning a lovely golden brown. She didn't stand out as a tourist quite as much now, but she certainly didn't look like a local either.

Jean turned to Angela, "there's plenty of room for us to sleep below and Jack won't want to sail when he's had a few drinks. There are two doubles, so we'll all be comfortable."

Angela quickly realised that unless she slept up on deck on her own, that she'd be sharing a bed with Jack. She wasn't very comfortable about it, but she wanted to be flexible or she'd ruin the day for everyone. She decided not to think about it until the time came. She liked Jack and she'd already noticed the chemistry between them but she wasn't looking for a holiday romance. Her life had been complicated enough over the past few months, so she'd have to try very hard to resist his charms. To be fair so far, he hadn't made any attempts to lure her. Maybe he was virtuous as his yacht? She hoped so.

They chatted for what felt like hours and eventually arrived in Dayan, which was as beautiful as Jack described. The water was the clearest blue that she'd ever seen and she wanted to jump straight in.

"Let's go and find the freshwater lake first," suggested Jack. "Wow, we couldn't have picked a better day for this and we made excellent time. We still have most of the day left." He put his hand out to Angela's and she found that she wanted to take it. She'd never experienced anything so natural before. There was something heavenly about Jack's touch which made her want to stay there. Holding back was no longer an option!

Jack led Angela towards the lake so that she could plunge straight into the cool water. It seemed obvious for them to jump, so they did. Angela felt the freedom of the whole of her being and she loved it. Her life was changing in miraculous ways and she was experiencing a new positivity that she hadn't felt for years.

Chapter 18 – Daisy

Daisy went up to her room to use her laptop. She'd asked her mum if she would take her to Brighton to meet her friends. She knew that she'd say no, because the only place her mother ever went was Norfolk, to see Grandma and Granddad, but it was worth a try.

"I'm sorry Daisy but we don't have the time. Any way you've got your A levels to think about. Aren't you meant to be studying? If you want any chance of going to university, you're going to have to try harder," said Linda.

"What A levels? You know I don't want to do them. I want to run a market stall so I won't need them. I'm not studying, so please don't go on about it. Dad goes on about it and I'm sick of it. If you can't take me to Brighton, then just say no. Don't say we haven't got time, because I'll get the train, bus, or something. I'll ask Dad for the money, not that he lets me do anything I want. I'm not staying there any more either, because he treats me like a baby. He makes me go to bed stupidly early. I'm an adult and should be able to go to bed when I like."

"You're nearly an adult Daisy, you're not an adult until you're eighteen and that's not until July. But ok, if we go to Norfolk again, you can stay here. I would prefer it if you came with us, or stayed with Gareth, but I understand it's boring for you because you can't see your friends. It will be better in the summer holidays because we can go to the beach. I will only leave you on one condition, that if I leave you for a weekend, you'll do some studying. Try and get English, if you can't manage History, or Art. Although, I thought you wanted Art the most?" asked Linda. She was fed up fighting Daisy but things were tough for her with two younger brothers and Gareth could give her a hard time. So, she tried to be patient.

"What I want is to go to Brighton, like the rest of my friends and I'll go even if I have to sell stuff," said Daisy sounding really annoyed. She didn't want to study, whatever the subject.

"Wait till your exams are over, then things will be easier. I don't understand why you have to go right now when it's not a good time," Linda continued. She didn't feel like getting into an argument when she had to get the boys. Daisy was being stubborn.

"It's never the right time though?" continued Daisy, throwing her hoody on to the floor and why is it so hot in here?"

The sun shone through the lounge windows and it had got very warm. The room faced south and when the sun came around it was surprising how much the temperature increased. The bruises on the top of Daisy's arm had faded but her mum hadn't noticed them because her arms were always covered. Even though her daughter was now wearing just a tee-shirt, Linda wasn't close enough to her to see the slight marks that remained. She was also way too tired most of the time to notice anything different.

"Daisy, I'm going to have to lie down until the boys finish at the sports centre."

"That makes a change? Why are you always running around after the boys and not me. You never ask me what I want to do? You always ignore me. It was worse when you lived with Dad, Gareth, or whatever he's called, Club. You didn't even know I was there. If you wanted me to do A levels then, you should've helped me with my school work years ago, but you were too interested in him, the man who hit you with a golf club," said Daisy, raising her voice. She had started to stomp around the room in a real rage because she was determined not to let this go. If she went on about it long enough, her mother would feel sorry for her and give her the money. She'd give in eventually, because it was easier than driving to Brighton.

"Daisy, that's enough. We've been through this already. I explained to you why I needed Gareth in my life and you said you understood. It's not true that I always put the boys first. It's just that they are young and they do a lot of sport. Their dad also takes them to football. We take it in turns. Ask your dad if you want to, but I expect he'll say no, because he's too selfish. At least I try?"

"Sometimes, but you're blind Mum and you don't often listen to me, even his girlfriend listens more than you do," continued Daisy.

"Girlfriend! Has Gareth got a new girlfriend?" asked Linda

"Yeah, and don't sound so surprised! I told you he's had loads to the house. This one's called Angela? She's a sports teacher and she's better than the rest. When I told her the truth about Dad, at least she believed me. Maybe she'll give me the money?"

"Don't be silly Daisy. You can't ask her. Even if she's nice, you don't know her. As I said, you can go in the summer, when your exams are over. You'll have saved up some money by then helping your friend on the market. The one who gives you the rings."

"Yeah, I might have, that's true," replied Daisy being careful not to say too much. Not that her Mum would realise she'd nicked the rings because she didn't know what day it was. Since Gareth left, and she'd started taking those pills, her mum had turned stupid. All she cared about were the boys. It was as if she lived in a trance.

I'm not going to be like that. I'm going to run my own business and forget this A level stuff. Why, care about university? Sarah loves me and I want to spend time with her. Sarah is sexually experienced and I'm ready for that now, Daisy thought, still angry at her Mum.

It was hard waiting when she needed to be part of Brighton's gay scene. At least there, she wouldn't feel like a freak. There was no gay scene here, well, there was her friend on the market but she wasn't a proper friend because she'd seriously pissed her off by charging too much for the rings.

Daisy loved silver. She collected it. One day she knew that she'd sell all her rings and she might have to do that soon if she couldn't get the fare. It was frustrating and she was angry. She wondered whether to tell her Mum she was gay but how the hell would she understand? Maybe one day she'd find out. If Gareth knew, he'd go bloody mad. He was a complete arse because he had such a stupid macho attitude towards women. She didn't care if she saw him again because it would be easier to come out. She needed to get some money from him first. If she pretended it was for another reason, like an extra exam, he'd pay for it. She'd have to have a think and work something out.

Angela cared, so maybe she'd help. At least she knew the truth about Gareth hitting her and that's more than her mum did. She didn't believe he'd hurt her. Her mum couldn't remember what he'd done to her! But she remembered every moment of it, seeing her mother covered with bruises while her brothers were screaming and finding somewhere to hide. That was when the bed wetting started, which went on and on until Gareth left.

God, she needed a spliff. She'd run out and was making do with herbs, which were half as good. She needed to get some before she phoned Angela, or she'd chicken out.

Daisy walked out of the door and headed for the market. There were a few people there who might help her out. She'd be home in a couple of hours, and then she'd message her mates to let them know she was coming. She had to meet Sarah. It was killing her!

Chapter 19 – Gareth

Gareth sent a text to Angela. When it arrived, she was in Dayan wallowing in a mud-filled pool with Jack, Jean and Alp, having the time of her life. They had started slinging mud at each other and it was everywhere, on their faces, in their hair and even in their mouths. Angela had started laughing and couldn't stop. This was the most fun she'd had in years. She was really happy and in no hurry to go anywhere. Her clothes were heaped on the top of a nearby sunbed and although she heard her mobile bleep, she wasn't moving. She couldn't hold her phone while she was caked in mud, which was spread over her arms, legs, bikini and face. When it cracked, she'd rinse it off in the lake. There was also a sulphur pool which was meant to help with all sorts of medical conditions, but Angela thought that it smelt vile and she had her limits!

"When we've finished here, we'll go and eat," declared Jack. I think that we'll save visiting the Lycian rock tombs and the ruins of the city until tomorrow because they're a bit of a trek. We'll want to eat and rest on Virtuous after this. I'm knackered!"

Angela couldn't believe the stunning scenery and

the variety of birds that flew around the lake. She was in awe of Turkey. She knew that it would be interesting but she had no idea how picturesque it was. There were breath-taking views of mountains and beautiful beaches along the Aegean coast, which supported all kinds of wildlife. When she was fully rinsed, she grabbed her towel and sat with it around her on a sun lounger. She finally took out her phone to see who had text and immediately noticed it was Gareth.

"Hi, have you returned from your holiday? Something terrible happened while you've been gone. Linda took an overdose and she's in hospital. The boys are staying with their grandparents for now and Daisy's with me. Can you pop over as soon as you get back because she's driving me nuts? Hope you're having fun." Gareth.

Angela returned her phone to her bag. She felt extremely anxious at the thought of Daisy staying with him until Linda was out of the hospital. It was hardly surprising that she kicked off. Her poor Mum. Why did she do that? Perhaps she was depressed. She'd have to see Gareth now, to make sure Daisy was alright. Damn, she was having such a great time here. She didn't want to think about his problems. He was involving her far too much!

"What's up? Not bad news I hope?" asked Jack noticing Angela's worried expression.

"Oh, it's ok. It's just this girl I know, she's having a few problems with her dad and I'm not sure what to do about it," she replied.

"Come and dissolve in the sulphur pool with me for a few minutes. It doesn't smell particularly good, but believe you me it clears your head," said Jack, as he took her hand again.

Angela didn't resist. She lay in the pool and cleansed. After a short time, she no longer noticed the smell. She'd deal with her problems when she returned, but right now, this dissolving was doing her good. Not only was it removing her worries but she felt as if it was lessening her resistance to Jack. Did she have to resist him? Maybe she should embrace it because he was such good company. He was also a great sailor who appeared to enjoy a challenge. She admired the way he navigated Virtuous and she'd noticed that he was always moving in the right direction. He appeared to be in control of his life and she loved his zest for it. She could learn a lot from his positive attitude.

When they finally emerged from the pool, they decided to look for some traditional Turkish food for an early dinner. As Angela ate her amazing meal, all she could think about was snuggling up with Jack. She felt both anticipation and excitement as she realised that she enjoyed his touch.

"Angela, what do you think of the local Turkish cuisine?" he asked, noticing that she was miles away.

"The food and the company are fantastic," she said, as she began to let down her guard.

"We'll dance later, and you can show me how to belly dance," Jack joked.

"Well, I can wiggle my hips but that's about it,

Angela replied, suddenly realising she was flirting.

"Hip wiggling works well here. If you join in with belly dancing, the girl will unbutton your skirt and show off your thighs. So, you better watch out!"

Angela laughed. She knew that her thighs were her best feature so why worry!

A few hours later, after a carafe of wine, she found herself doing just that, dancing as she'd never danced before, whilst Jack received a prize view of her shapely legs. They all danced for hours. They were the last four people in the restaurant. Then they returned to Virtuous to watch the full moon, as it shone on the water.

The four of them were completely exhausted after such a brilliant night. First the meal, later sunbathing on the yacht, then more swimming and the endless dancing.

"Angela, you're such great fun when you relax. Have you got a problem bunking up with me tonight, so we can give the two love birds a little space?" asked Jack?"

"Well, it wasn't part of my plan but I guess there's no harm in it. I guess my other choice is to sleep on my own, up on the deck, which could get a bit chilly during the night,"

"Or, we could take the bed up on deck and look at the stars together?" suggested Jack, smiling.

"That would be magic. What a wonderful idea!"

Half an hour later, Jack and Angela laid on top of a duvet with dozens of cushions underneath. They had a thick blanket over them and they were still both fully dressed. Angela put her head into the crook of Jack's arm. He pointed at the various star formations. The Plough, the Dipper and the Bear. Although Angela was a keen stargazer, she was surprised by Jack's knowledge, so she kept quiet and listened to him.

"You know that you're the first and only woman I've done this with," he said in a whisper.

"Really, well thank you Jack. I'm having such a wonderful time. I don't want to go home because Turkey feels like my spiritual home."

"Perhaps it is. Sometimes things fall into place with very little effort and other times we give it our all and it's still not right."

For a moment Angela thought Jack was talking about him and Jean. She detected a slight note of sadness in his voice. She snuggled closer and he put his arm around her. The next moment, Angela felt Jack's lips tenderly caressing her mouth. It felt both beautiful and exciting. She soon began to feel aroused by this knowledgeable and charming man. He slid his arms around her to hold her tight.

"Goodnight," he said as he stroked her hair.

She soon fell into a peaceful sleep while listening to the sound of Jack's heart, along with the rushing of the waves. Virtuous continued to rock gently in the breeze.

Angela awoke at seven thirty to find that she was sleeping on her side with Jack's arms around her. He was breathing deeply and she assumed that he was asleep. She smiled and slowly pulled away from him.

She jumped up, straightened her clothes and looked for a mirror to straighten her hair.

The sun was already shining on one half of Virtuous and she knew that it would soon come around to cover the complete deck. There was no noise from below, so she guessed that Jean and Alp were also asleep. She sat down on the seat on the edge of the deck and gazed into the water. It was so clear. It looked to be about twenty-foot deep and she could just about see the sand at the bottom. It was an incredible experience. The sea was a stunning azure blue! Her eyes needed protecting from the strong sun so she put on her sun glasses and applied her sun cream.

Angela was now a beautiful shade of brown but she didn't want to be complacent about it. The sun had often caught her out and she needed to take care. She was aware she looked different because part of her had awakened in this beautiful country. Turkey, she would come back here again. Perhaps she'd come when her sons had finished their exams before the main summer holidays, then, it might be slightly cheaper. Marcus and Shaun deserved a treat. Both of them had been studying so hard that it would be good for them. They planned to visit the tombs today and later return to Marmaris. Jean and Alp had planned trips for the rest of the week which included Jack. Angela was pleased that she could see him for a while longer because he made her feel so comfortable. She thought about how they snuggled up together, looked at the stars and how he'd kissed her. She had never been kissed like that before. It was neither demanding, nor urgent but it was friendly, definite and enjoyable. Jack could easily have taken advantage of her last night because she had drunk so much wine, but he hadn't. It was a challenge for her to get up and belly dance and she'd drunk a carafe of wine to find the courage. This morning she felt dehydrated and she reached for her water bottle.

Jack started to stir, and sat up abruptly.

"Angela, you're up bright and early. I hope you enjoyed looking at the stars last night, I certainly did. We'll go and see the tombs after breakfast, you'll love them. There's so much history in this ancient land. Your week's going so fast, you'll need to stay longer," he said, smiling.

"Sadly, I can't stay any longer. I wish I could, but I'll come back with my boys. We need to get their exams out of the way first, and when school finishes for the summer, who knows. The world is my oyster," she said, feeling flattered that Jack wanted her to stay.

Jean and Alp appeared to say the coffee was on and they had made breakfast. They warned that they had to take plenty of water today because it was even hotter, 33 degrees, and they'd be walking.

Jean suddenly said, "So what happened to you two last night? I peeped in to say goodnight and neither of you were there. Did you go for a midnight swim, or shall I say a 1 am swim?"

"No, we didn't swim. We lay under the stars," said

Jack, smiling at Jean.

"Lay under the stars," she said very quietly. For a moment Angela noticed a look on Jean's face that she'd never seen before. It could have been curiosity or jealousy; she wasn't really sure but it made her feel a little uncomfortable."

"What did the stars tell you?" Jean continued, sensing that Angela had observed her expression. Jean was now trying to make light of it by being friendly.

"They said that sometimes we make mistakes, but we must forgive ourselves and move on. They also said that when I get home, I'm going to receive some good news," Angela replied smiling.

"Really?" said Jean.

"Yes, really, because by saying it. I'm creating it."

"Ah, a bit like my number plate. You're getting the hang of it," said Jean who suddenly looked her old self again.

Jack looked at the two women curiously. They spoke a special language he didn't understand.

"I'm not sure that I have, but we need to make tracks soon, or Angela will miss out," said Jack, as he attempted to clear away the remains of their breakfast.

Alp looked at them curiously and smiled. He already knew that his luck had changed when he met Jean. The woman he to planned marry. He didn't need any stars to tell him that. It was simple, she had a beautiful body and they made love for hours on end and that's what he wanted. He smiled at Jean and squeezed her backside. She wasn't embarrassed by him and she ran her hands over the top of his muscular arms while giving him a kiss on the lips.

"Right, let's go then," said Angela, quickly turning away. How she ached for Jack to touch her like that but she knew that it wasn't the right time, not yet. She had to finish her relationship with Gareth first and tie up some other loose ends.

"I'll be here for you when you return," said Jack, when they eventually reached the tombs.

"I'd like that, because we're a long time dead" she replied, looking for Jack's hand. As he once again took her hand in his, Angela felt as if it would take the whole of her weight, her body, mind and soul. Despite this, she realised that for now, she had to carry her own weight, which she knew she would do like a Goddess.

Chapter 20 – Marcus

Angela arrived home a few days later and was greeted by Marcus.

"Of course, we missed you, Mum, but guess what, I've got a letter to say that I've been accepted into university!" said Marcus, who was absolutely beaming.

"Wow, that's fantastic! Well done, I can't believe it. Have you told your dad?" asked Angela.

"Well, the letter came when you were in Turkey. I guessed what it was, so I opened it with Dad because he was here. I couldn't wait until you came home so that I could share the news with you as well," he explained.

"I'm glad that you've got in somewhere. Which one is it? Come on, tell me, I'm so excited for you."

"Birmingham, which is fantastic because it's only a few hours from here and you'll be able to come and see me," said Marcus.

"Birmingham, wow, I can't believe it. How exciting. It's a brand-new start for you. I had such a fantastic time in Turkey. Jean said that I can bring both of you with me next time. So, we'll do that, shall we? When you've both finished your exams? I guess going to Birmingham, is dependent on your grades, but we'll know soon enough and I think you'll get what you want," Angela said, encouragingly.

"It's such a high standard Mum. I tried my best, but who knows," replied Marcus.

"Whatever your results turn out to be, I'm proud of you for working so hard. Come here and give me a hug," she asked.

Marcus came over. He was tall blonde and very good looking. He made Angela feel tiny in comparison. I'm going to go out for a run soon. Would you like to come with me, then we can go out for a drink to celebrate?

"Yes, that sounds great but I don't want to be too long, because I've got a pile of things to do."

"Agreed," said Angela smiling. She couldn't believe it. It was absolutely amazing, far better than she expected. She ran upstairs and looked for her running shorts and realised that she hadn't even unpacked from her holiday but she wanted to run. She thought how strange it was that she made a declaration on holiday about good news coming and when she returned home it happened.

Angela ran out of the house with Marcus and they headed to the park. Her son was fit and she struggled to keep up with him.

"I knew that I was going to get in somewhere soon because I saw four magpies sitting on the lawn, then the letter arrived," said Marcus, laughing.

"Four, I've never seen four together, that's incredible."

"Yes, I had to blink twice. I told them that I'm not a boy but I appreciated their gesture," he said, laughing.

Angela laughed too. Then she suddenly became serious. "You're right. You're definitely not a boy, but you are my brilliant son. Right, I'll race you back home because then we'll still have a bit of time left to go for that drink. Then, I've got a few important phone calls to make," she continued, with a little trepidation.

Once Marcus had gone, she decided to give Gareth a quick call to let him know she was back. She wanted to see how he was getting on with Daisy and if she could do anything to help. She was home now, so she might as well be friendly. It was a short-term solution until Daisy was safe.

"Hi Gareth, it's Angela, I got back late last night so I thought I'd give you a quick call," she said, feeling uneasy in the pit of her stomach.

"Angela, fantastic. I'm so glad you're back. I've been having problems with Daisy since Linda had the breakdown. I've been going to and from to look after their cat. Daisy wanted to stay on her own. Apparently, Linda told her she could, but I wasn't told so I said no to her and she kicked off. I also had to take the boys out of school for a week but they're staying with their grandparents now. I'm still going to work because Daisy's only left on her own for a few hours, and she's old enough for that. I don't know what's going on with her but some girl called at the house last night. Her friend from the market?

I heard them shouting in the hallway and the girl accused her of stealing her rings, something about she saw them for sale online! The girl went crazy and started laying into Daisy, so I had to separate them. I could smell weed so she's probably supplying Daisy. I don't know what goes on at that market, but I think Daisy's been pulling the wool over Linda's eyes because she's been stealing. I took a peep in her room, I promised I wouldn't, but I was worried. There was silver jewellery all over the place. It looks like she's been running a business. Some of it she could have bought herself, but the five silver rings, I'm not sure about. She's like a Magpie. She hoards everything, especially silver but it's got beyond a joke! She seems to have a weird addiction to it. I don't want to get mad at her until I've spoken to her mother. She could have bought some of the stuff," explained Gareth, who was fuming.

"Five silver rings," repeated Angela. For a minute, she wanted to laugh. She wanted to say 'isn't it meant to be five gold rings', but she thought Gareth would explode! She needed to get a grip and be serious. She continued, "Gareth, I know that you're mad, but Daisy is only seventeen and it must be hard having a mother who's sick most of the time. Would you like me to talk to her? Perhaps I could get through and find out what's going on?"

"No Angela, I don't want you to talk to her. You can come over but, not being rude, it's really my problem. I can sort it out. When I confronted her, she said, they were her rings and she had to sell them because she needed the money. I just hope that she isn't going to disappear on me because that's all I need, a runaway teenage daughter."

"She's seventeen Gareth, and she's doing her A levels so she's hardly likely to run away! Even if she went, she's not a baby. I thought she was quite grown up. She looked after me when I came around, the time you were late back from London," said Angela, in an effort to calm him down. Angela didn't understand why he would text her on holiday sounding like he needed help, then push her away!

"But she doesn't want to do her A levels. I don't know whether she bothered to turn up for the exams. She might have bunked off. How the hell do I know what she's up to? Linda is obviously useless at keeping her under control. I might have to ground her at weekends until I can get to the bottom of this. What else has she been hiding from me? No more trips to that bloody market because it's obviously where all the trouble started. Stealing, smoking weed and hanging out with unsavory types? Next thing you know, she'll be pregnant," he said, raising his voice.

"I don't think so, Gareth."

"What do you mean. You don't think so? How can you be so sure?"

Because I think Daisy is gay, well likes girls."

"Gay, you're kidding me! Angela, my daughter isn't gay. Anyway, how the hell do you know when you've only spoken to her a couple of times. I know you're a teacher, but that doesn't give you the right to make judgements about my family. Are your sons gay?"

"I wasn't making a judgement, Gareth and as far as I know, my sons aren't gay, but if they were, I wouldn't have a problem with it."

"Then, if that wasn't a judgement, what the hell was it?"

"I was merely saying that it was a possibility, something I just felt."

"Felt. Like it's going to piss down with rain tomorrow. I wish you'd think before you open your mouth," he said, mocking her.

"I've got to go now, Gareth. I was going to tell you about my good news but you're obviously not up to listening. I know you're angry, but please don't take it out on me. I've just got back from holiday and I was ringing to see if I could help. I don't need your anger because I've got loads of things to sort out before I go back to work."

"Hey Angela, I'm really sorry. I tell you what; I'll cook dinner soon. Let me get this stuff out of the way with Daisy, then I promise, I'll make some time for you," he replied, completely changing his tone.

Angela didn't know what to say. She didn't want to encourage him by letting him think that she wanted to get deeper into the relationship, but she felt drawn to him like a spider to a web. She decided that for now, the best plan was to say something casual, which was neither yes nor no!

"Ok then, when I've caught up with my paperwork."

"Great. I've missed you, Angela. You only went for a week, but it felt like ages."

Angela was surprised that Gareth missed her when they had hardly dated and he was always working in London or off playing golf. She suddenly realised that she could pop over to see Daisy one day after school while he was working. It would be a lot easier to talk on their own. She had to see if the girl was alright. She'd had another dream last night about her sobbing but this time she was hugging and reassuring her everything would be ok. Daisy told her that Gareth had picked up a golf club again and threatened her with it. She was scared that he was going to beat her the same way he did her mother.

Angela woke from the dream in the early hours of the morning with sweat pouring off her. It felt like a warning. She'd started taking more notice of her intuition and following the signs when something didn't feel right. It was as if the Magpies were trying to tell her something. It was the same when she saw one the day Martin died. Were the magpies real, or imaginary? It was strange that Marcus also saw four, when he received his news.

"Angela, are you there because I can't hear you? Am I talking to myself?" asked Gareth in an impatient tone.

"No, I'm still listening but I have to go. See you soon," she said abruptly and turned off her mobile. She'd pop by to see Daisy on Monday, after work. It might be her only chance.

Chapter 21 – Sally

When Angela arrived at the school on Monday morning, it looked very different. The atmosphere was calm and the pupils seemed relatively happy. As she walked into the staff room, Sally walked over to greet her.

"Hello Angela, we've missed you," Sally said, in a positive tone.

"Hello Sally, I can't believe that I'm back at work, so quickly. Everything looks so tidy and organised. Have there been any major problems whilst I've been gone?" she asked.

"No, and to be honest, I'm enjoying being head. I've taken up residence in Martin's old office after the Police said it was alright to do so. I have better access to the information in his filing cabinets. The old desk has gone. We've got a great new one now, with new keys. I've got one and there is one in the key cupboard. No more secrets," she said, giving Angela a tiny smile.

"Great, a new start for all of us then. I don't want to think about what happened because I've had such a lovely holiday. I'll tell you about it over lunch if you're able to take a break? It will be great to catch up."

"Angela, you look radiant. Whatever happened while you were in Turkey obviously did you the world of good. Look how brown you are and you're looking very fit," said Sally.

"Well, I managed to get in a few runs in over the holiday, so I will be more on form this term. The really excellent news is that Marcus got into Birmingham University to do Sports Science. It was such a fantastic surprise when I returned home. I was a little sad that I missed him opening the letter, but does that matter. It's amazing," she said, excitedly.

"That's great news but I've got to rush now because I'm meant to be supervising a class this morning. The teacher is off sick. I'll catch up with you at lunchtime. Pop by and see the new look office, you'll love it. There are also some new plants," she explained excitedly.

"I will," she replied, then she made her way down to the gym for her first lesson. To her surprise, she found herself looking forward to it.

The day passed quickly. Angela had a great lunch catching up with Sally and there were even a few giggles over the change of desk. Not what they found in the drawers but about their more intimate moments with Martin.

"Did you enjoy it, though?" asked Sally, smiling.

"No, I didn't. The heating was off, I was freezing, and it was very uncomfortable. How about you?"

"It was different but I'm so glad that man is out of my life. I'm not saying that I don't think what happened was absolutely tragic but now that I've got into this job, I'm finding that I don't miss him. That sounds a little cruel, but I feel this was meant to be. I was originally looking for a Head Teacher's position, but as I didn't get either of the jobs I applied for, I gave up and went for Deputy Head. I love the Head's job. The challenge of turning the school around and making it more 21st Century, is brilliant," Sally said smiling.

Angela agreed the school did need updating and Sally appeared to be the woman for the job. She was bored with teaching and she needed change and things would change for her when both of her sons were settled.

It was now 4 pm and Angela walked to her car. She messaged the boys to say that she was going to be a little late because she needed to visit someone. They offered to start dinner, which helped her to feel more relaxed. She knew that they would prefer to do that than to wait.

Angela arrived at Gareth's house at 4.20 pm. She was unsure if Daisy would be there but Gareth gave her the impression that she was staying at his house in the week. She hastily knocked on the door and stood back, to wait for Daisy to answer. There was no answer for ages, so Angela gently pushed open the letterbox and peered in. Loud rock music greeted her then she noticed Daisy coming down the stairs. She quickly stood back so Daisy couldn't see her looking through the glass.

"Yeah," said a voice through the door.

"It's me, Angela. I've popped by to see if you're

ok."

"I don't want to see anyone," she replied, adamantly.

"Daisy, listen, I need to know if you are ok. Can you at least give me a few minutes and open the door," she asked.

"What do you want because Dad's not here," she replied, gruffly.

"I don't want your dad. I need to know that you're ok. I've been really worried about you since I saw the marks on your arms. You can talk to me or you can talk to the Police, but I can't just leave this," said Angela.

"Daisy opened the door. Her eyes looked black as if she hadn't slept for weeks. She also looked quite thin. She wore a long black tee shirt and jeans with various rips in them. Angela was shocked by her gaunt expression and she wanted to hug her but she knew that she'd probably close up."

"Dad and I had a huge row last night, about the rings. My mate from the market came over and said I stole them from her and he heard us talking. I was trying to sell the rings so I can go and see my friend Sarah, who lives in Brighton. I'll get a train, but now that's all gone wrong. As usual, I don't get to go where I want," said Daisy.

"So, you want to go to Brighton to meet Sarah?" pressed Angela.

"Yeah, and get away from my mad father. The one who says he's my dad when he isn't. He got so mad last night that he pushed me up against the lounge wall. He had his hand on my throat and I was terrified. I thought he was going to strangle me. I managed to kick him in the shin and he let go. I said that I'd scream so loud, the neighbours would hear if he came anywhere near me again, so he stopped. But a few minutes later he went for one of his golf clubs. When I started screaming, he put it back again. I've got to get away from here because he's mad. He did this to Mum and look what happened to her. She's on all sorts of meds because of him," said Daisy as she started to cry.

Angela still wanted to hold her, but she wasn't going to step over that line. She quickly walked into the kitchen and Daisy followed. She filled up the kettle and said, "time for me to make you a cup of tea because we need to plan."

Angela took some sips of tea and she noticed that Daisy started to drink as well. Angela had put three sugars in Daisy's tea to help her with shock. They both stood leaning on the worktop not wishing to get too comfortable because they knew Gareth would return shortly.

"Daisy, you need to get away from Gareth. I understand about the money and why you want to sell the rings, but you need help right now. Let me see if I can help, but you will have to trust me on this and do what I ask. Don't say anything at all to Gareth. For the time being, I will pretend that there's nothing wrong. We will get you away from here, I promise.

Here, have this necklace and earrings, they're Italian gold and I've had them for years. Sell them and put the money into your savings account. I don't need them anymore."

Daisy looked at Angela in total disbelief. "Really, that's amazing thank you. It's my birthday in a few weeks' time and I'll be eighteen, so no-one will be able to tell me what to do then."

"Well, maybe wait until then. These last few weeks of term will fly past and then, freedom. Just hang on in their Daisy and keep in touch. I'm sure you'll get to meet Sarah soon."

Angela said goodbye feeling reassured that the girl was listening to her and that she'd have money to travel. It made sense for her to wait until her birthday and hopefully she'd seen the light about this. Angela got into her car and drove home to discover that her sons had the dinner ready for her.

"I'm booking the flight for our holiday because the prices are good at the moment," she said, decisively.

"Really. That's amazing. I can't wait," said Shaun.

"Neither can I! It will be brilliant fun, staying with Jean and her boyfriend. You said they've got a pool, that's fantastic," said Marcus.

"Yes, there's a pool and the sea's only a short distance away. It's the bluest sea that you'll ever see with fantastic beaches. You will find the harbour interesting too and you'll be able to meet my friend Jack. He's got an incredible yacht which he keeps at the Marina. In fact, there are a lot of yachts there. Marmaris is a great place. You won't be bored," said Angela who was feeling excited all over again. Jack had actually texted her earlier that day. It simply said

I'm waiting for you!' to which she replied 'I'm only just home, but I'm dying to return with my family.'

Angela thought about Jack most of the time. That week had gone so quickly, yet in some way, she felt as if she had known him longer than she'd known Gareth, which was strange. What would she do about Gareth's invitation to dinner? Did he expect to have sex with her? She didn't want to give herself to him. The thought of sex with him terrified her. She needed to focus her energies on her work and look forward to seeing Jack when she returned to Turkey. She tried not to compare them because it made things complicated in her head. Gareth was history, but part of her was still living it out! It felt like a karmic experience they were still working out! She didn't want this lesson, but whatever they had to learn, they were stuck in it together!

Angela knuckled down to work. Since Sally had run the school, her sessions seemed to run like clockwork. The children were in the right place at the right time and they were keen about their lessons because they understood what was going on!

She'd also found that she had so much energy since she'd returned from Turkey. Most mornings she went for a short run before work. Sometimes Marcus joined her because he was aware of the level of fitness he needed for university. Other times, Shaun came with her, but not often because he wasn't really into running. Shaun loved football and he hoped to turn professional at some stage. Angela knew that both her sons were very ambitious and she tried to support them as much as possible. It was difficult juggling so many different things, work, their school work, cleaning the house, keeping fit and healthy. The list went on and on.

Two weeks passed and one evening out of the blue, she got that call from Gareth asking her around to dinner on Saturday evening. He told her that Linda was out of the hospital and he didn't have Daisy or the boys. He was going to cook something special. He couldn't wait to see her because it was the first time in ages that he had a completely free evening!

Angela was in half a mind to say no, then she remembered her promise to Daisy about appearing normal, so that Gareth wouldn't take his temper out on her. Plus, it was such a short period of time until the girl was eighteen. She would soon be free to do as she pleased.

"Ok then. I'll be at yours for 7 pm, on Saturday," she replied.

"You don't sound very keen. Is there something wrong?" he asked.

"No, nothing's wrong. It's just that I've been bogged down with work lately and I'm trying to catch up. I'm looking forward to it," she lied. The truth was that she felt sick to her stomach. The idea of spending time alone with a man who had grabbed his daughter by the throat was absolutely terrifying. She went to fetch a glass of water to try to calm down. She wasn't going to do anything to wind him up. Her phone would be left on and she'd tell a few friends where she was going. With her working out each day plus the running, she was probably as strong as him?

Chapter 22 – The Meal

Angela got ready for her date with Gareth. She told her sons that she would be back but probably not until about twelve and she was going to see a girlfriend. They were fine with that because they had their friends around at the weekends, so they didn't go to bed early. She knew that she could trust them and there were a few cans of beer in the fridge. She thought about taking some wine with her but decided that it was too much of a risk. If she drank, she wouldn't be able to drive home. She wanted to be friendly and polite but not to compromise herself in any way. It would be difficult. She wasn't sure what she'd say but hopefully when it got to around eleven pm, she'd find an excuse and leave.

The journey to Gareth's house was quicker than expected and she very soon walked up to his front door. Gareth opened the door and to her surprise, he was wearing a dinner jacket. Angela was stunned. She felt underdressed in black jeans and a jumper but she had no idea he was going to do this.

"Come in Angela; let me take your coat. You look nice, he said admiring her outfit. "Oh, you're not wearing those nice gold earrings tonight," he said gently brushing back her hair with his fingers to take a closer look.

"Ah no, I decided they reminded me of my ex, so I've given them to a friend," she said.

"A friend. A lucky friend because they looked expensive but I guess you're right. It's sometimes good to move things on and not think about their value," he said, smiling.

"Gareth, I feel underdressed. I had no idea that you were going to this amount of trouble. You look amazing in that jacket and I would have worn an evening dress had I known."

"Please don't worry. Dressing up was my choice. I saw it hanging up in the cupboard and I thought it's wasted in there, so I decided to give the old boy an airing," he replied confidently.

He led her into the dining room, where he'd gone to a similar amount of trouble with the table decorations and candles.

"Wow, I'm impressed," Angela said. "What a beautiful table arrangement." For a moment the whole vision took her breath away. It was hard to believe that this charming man, only a few weeks ago, had his daughter by the throat up against the lounge wall. Part of her wanted to disbelieve Daisy, because she remembered the great sex they'd shared and felt a tinge of sadness. Why did this have to happen? What had she done to deserve this situation and how on earth was she going to get clear of it?

"Sit down Angela. I'll pour us some wine, which is one of your favourites and you can tell me about your day. I want to hear about how your son got into university? Is that what you were going to tell me?" He said, suddenly appearing very interested.

"That seems like ages ago now. Marcus got into Birmingham to do a degree in Sports Science. I'm very proud of him. We'll find out about his A level grades any day now, then we'll know if he can definitely go. I'm sure he'll get what he needs, but it's been tough.

"Yeah, it's tough for kids now. I don't know if Daisy attended her exams. She said she did, but who knows if she's telling the truth! Anyway, her mother is home now and she's staying with her for a few days. It's probably just as well because she drove me completely mad. It's one thing having her for the odd weekend, but living with me is a definite no. Her real dad's useless or she could have stayed with him. I don't know where he is now because he travels around London and abroad. He's into some really dodgy stuff.

"The dinner smells good," said Angela, changing the subject.

"Yes, I made us a vegetarian casserole it's different but I'm sure you'll like it. Would you like a top-up?", he asked as he leaned over to refill her glass.

"No, that's ok. I can't drink much tonight because I took some painkillers." It was the easiest thing for her to say, on the spur of the moment.

"Oh, I hope you're not in pain?"

"It's my back. I pulled a muscle running, early this

morning, twisting awkwardly."

"Well, let's have the food. I can give you a massage later?" he said, smiling.

Angela imagined Gareth's hands on her body and she couldn't help but feel a little excited. The wine had numbed her senses slightly and all she could think about was how absolutely amazing he looked in a dinner jacket. She needed to remind herself what she was dealing with here but it was hard. Part of her wanted to dismiss her earlier thoughts about being on her guard and be in the moment.

"Angela, I've been meaning to tell you that I was sorry about talking so much about my family problems. Tell me about your holiday. What did you do? You said you stayed with Jean, the friend you met at university? What else happened there? I saw on the internet that Marmaris is a great place for yachts. Did you manage to get in any sailing or diving?" he asked.

"We went out on a friend's yacht for a day trip to an incredible bay. We also visited some mud baths, that was a bit of a laugh. Oh yes, and we saw some ancient tombs," she added in a matter-of-fact way.

"So, you mummified yourselves, did you?" asked Gareth, laughing.

"Not mummified because I do enough of that at home," she replied, joining in with the joke. They chatted for a while about her trip but she was careful not to mention Jack. Gareth appeared interested but he later began to talk about how he had won another trophy whilst she was on holiday.

"Look, it's in that cabinet over there, right at the front," he said, pointing it out.

Angela looked over to a large gold cup. "Wonderful," she whispered trying not to sound sarcastic.

When they'd finished dinner, Gareth cleared the plates and she helped him. They then shared some cheese biscuits and grapes which were laid out on the coffee table.

"I've missed you," he said putting his arm around her shoulders. "I suppose I better take this jacket off now before it gets ruined," he said slinging it over a chair.

Angela got up from the sofa and looked at her watch.

"What's the matter now? It's only nine and we've still got hours."

"I can't stay long because I need to be home for tonight," she said tentatively.

"What, again! Can't you give them a ring or something, or send a text to say that you won't be back until the morning?"

"No, not really," she replied. Angela suddenly felt very alarmed by the tone of Gareth's voice.

"Angela, I've missed you and I wanted tonight to be special because I don't have the kids. I was also going to rub your back, wasn't I? Even if you don't stay the night, you'll let me do that for you, won't you?"

Angela sat down on the sofa and placed her mobile phone on the coffee table. She turned it off because she knew she would keep checking the time. There was a wall clock at the other end of the lounge so she could glance discreetly at that. He asked her where it hurt and she told him it ached across her shoulders.

"Lie down then," Gareth said in a voice which she thought sounded like an order.

"I've just eaten.

"That was over an hour ago."

"Lie down please Angela," he repeated.

Angela removed her top but kept her bra on and she lay on her front on the sofa. Gareth knelt down next to her and started to rub her back gently between her shoulder blades. She began to relax and even feel a little sleepy. She found the mixture of food, wine and fatigue made her want to let go. Although she'd been careful and only drank one glass.

"I need to go now," she said, ten minutes later. She realised that the longer she stayed there, the harder it would be to get up and go.

"I haven't finished yet. Please lie still," said Gareth, sounding annoyed as she went to move away.

"I'm really ready to go now," she repeated.

Angela struggled to get up from the sofa because Gareth sat on the side of it blocking her way. He then climbed on to her back and straddled her. She felt as if she couldn't breathe.

"Gareth, don't do that. You're squashing me. Get off," she demanded.

To her relief, she felt Gareth remove his weight. She was just about to get to her feet when she suddenly felt a searing pain across her back. As she turned her body to stand up, she saw Gareth holding a raised golf club.

"You bitch Angela. You deserve it. And if you come round to speak to my daughter again, I will beat you so badly that those beautiful thighs won't run again. Who the hell do you think you are? Did you think I wouldn't know what you were up to? My neighbours keep me informed of anyone unusual who comes to the house. Now get out of here while you still can," he shouted as he dropped the metal club to the floor.

Angela grabbed her phone and bag, leaving her coat and headed for the front door. She could still hear Gareth shouting "I'll give you five seconds to leave." As she ran to her car, her heart was beating uncontrollably. The fear inside her was causing her to sweat profusely. Her back was agony and tears rapidly streamed down her face.

Oh my God, Daisy, she thought and her poor mum. The man was completely mad. She wasn't going to his house ever again. She needed to drive straight to the Police. As she headed towards the Police station, she realised that she realised her phone was on because she suddenly received a text, which made her heart stop. She kept driving until she came to a bus stop where she pulled in to read it. Surprisingly it was from Daisy. It said "Angela, don't go and see my dad, because he found out about your visit and said he was going to kill you. I hope you get this in time! I'm going to Brighton soon. I'm not sure what Mum's going to do and I'm worried about her. I managed to sell the gold jewellery you gave me. Thanks for helping me. Daisy x

Angela rushed home. She was still in shock and the pain from her back was excruciating. She decided not to go to the Police Station because she was in too much pain. It was going to be hard for her to put a brave face on for the boys when all she wanted to do was to hide away but she had to face them.

At long last, she burst in through the front door avoiding Silver. She'd asked Marcus to feed him because his dishes were empty. "I'm sorry but I feel so ill," she said, limping up the stairs. She quickly ran a warm deep bath and slowly got in. There were some drops of blood in the water and she realised Gareth had broken her skin. She was in extreme shock and felt sick. As she lay in the bath, there was a voice at the door. It was Marcus. "Mum, are you alright? What happened? You didn't have a crash, did you?"

Angela thought for a moment. "No, I slipped on my friend's drive and landed on my back on some sharp stones. I'm in a lot of pain and I need to see the Doctor but please don't worry about me. I'm just going to stay in the bath for a while then I'll lie down."

"Ok Mum, but if you want anything please give me a call," he said.

"Just feed the cat, please," she shouted as he walked away.

Angela was overwhelmed with sadness and started to cry. First, for the pain she was in, and secondly for Daisy and her mother. Why do people behave like this? She wondered what else Linda had been through. She found it hard to believe that no-one believed her and it became a joke! It was appalling. Angela was horrified by Gareth's behaviour, firstly he was pretending that they were going to have a wonderful evening together, then suddenly his attitude changed and he became a different person. She was lucky to get away. It could have been a lot worse if she'd frozen to the spot. Fortunately, she had a huge rush of adrenalin which made her run. Obviously, Daisy wasn't so lucky when Gareth pinned her to the wall. She felt dreadful for doubting her story because the girl was obviously telling the truth. What a shame she had to experience it first hand, to believe her! If her phone had been on, she'd have received her text and left earlier.

Angela opened the bathroom cabinet and found a small bottle of rescue remedy, which she always used for shock. She took it and within about ten minutes, she started to feel a little better. She decided that even though it was late, she'd telephone Jean. She needed support because she was still very shaken up.

"Angela, the man's mad and you say that he's got children? Oh my God. You must report him to the police because that's assault. Just think of what he might do to Daisy!" said Jean, who was horrified.

"I know that, but Gareth is a very clever man and if I go to the Police, he may do something to his children out of anger. He's obviously a violent man. I can't believe I fell for someone like him. I must be very stupid. He seemed so kind, caring and interesting. Well, I've really had enough of the UK now. Not a single thing has gone right for me over the last year. It started when I met Martin and since then I feel like I've been going downhill. I must admit Sally's doing a fantastic job running the school. My lessons seem to run like clockwork but in all honesty, I don't want to be there. I wish I could do something different, anything, as long as it's not teaching sport."

"Then do it. Don't just talk about it. I got out and look at my life now. I live in a gorgeous place I have a beautiful house and a brilliant lover. What more could I ask for? I admit I'd like to see my children more but they come when they can and when they do, it's fantastic," replied Jean.

"Would you like to swop?" Angela said, a bit tongue in cheek. There was a long silence from Jean on the phone and then Jean replied cheerfully,

"Come next week because we haven't got any family staying then and bring the boys if they've finished their exams. I've got loads of room here. It's going to get busier when the school holidays come, so come and stay longer this time. In fact, stay for the summer. Alp can sort you out a separate villa if we get full. He's got loads of friends who can help, or we can ask Jack."

Angela sat propped against some pillows while she was talking to Jean. Her back still hurt. She wanted to look at her injuries in her full-length mirror but something made her too scared to look. Seeing the damage might make it hurt more. It would definitely make the pain of her ignorance worse, which was something she couldn't face.

"We'll come. I'll tell Sally that I have to finish school a week early. She won't be pleased but I have to get away from here soon," she said, suddenly regaining a bit of strength and determination.

"That's my Ang. Let me know what time you'll get to the airport so we can come pick you all up," said Jean.

"I will. Thank God, I met you, Jean." she replied, then took a very long breath.

Chapter 23 – The Next day and Ready to Go

"So, we're going to Turkey at the end of next week and we're spending the summer there. I spoke to your dad and he's fine about it. Jean can put us up for a few weeks and after that, we'll rent our own villa. I can't see that's a problem because Jean has so many contacts," said Angela, enthusiastically. Her sons looked amazed but they also appeared excited.

"We're going that soon? That's brilliant Mum. How did you get the last week off school?"

"I phoned Sally and told her that I won't be back this term because of my back injury. The Doctor wrote me off sick for two weeks this morning. He said that I should feel better in a week and he's given me some stronger pain killers. I'll see him again before we go. Sally's going to get in a supply teacher until the end of the term."

"Wicked," said Shaun, who was already looking up Turkey on google maps? "It looks like there's loads to do in Marmaris, Mum and the beach looks amazing."

"Yes, it is amazing. You'll both love it and you won't be bored."

"So, do we get to go on this posh yacht that you told us about?" asked Marcus, grinning.

"Yes, I hope so, but we'll have to see because Jack likes to travel, so he might be away. Can you please look for your passports and start making a list of things to take? There won't be that much room in Jean's car so please pack small suitcases, not large ones. I'm going to take a rest for a few hours. I'll pop into town for more holiday supplies a bit later," said Angela. She felt relieved by her sons' positive reaction to her news.

Angela went upstairs to lie down. Her back was still very uncomfortable and she noticed that the bruising had started to come out. She felt sure that the new pain killers would kick in soon. Just as she rested her head on the pillow, she noticed a text come in from Gareth. As she opened it, her hands shook, this was the last thing she needed.

Hi Angela, just to let you know that if you go to the Police, I'll do the same to Daisy as I did to you, or worse. You had a lucky escape this time but if you come near my family again, there will be trouble. Don't think about grassing me up because I have golf friends in the Police. It's a shame that you didn't do what I asked because you were such a good fuck. Still, you can't win them all. Daisy isn't allowed to contact you but if she does, I will report her for stealing from the market.

Angela, read the text twice. It was long and she had to scroll up. Why would he say such a thing to Daisy? Gareth was blackmailing her. She realised that he must be psychologically sick and need help. He obviously enjoyed making people suffer by controlling and manipulating them. Angela knew she had to do something about this, but what? She was extremely frightened of him since the golf club incident and she wanted to keep away.

Angela breathed, stretched out on her bed and soon fell to sleep. She awoke to the sound of her alarm, which she'd set on her phone for about an hour later. Surprisingly, despite Gareth's threats, she saw a text from Daisy which read, Hi Angela I'm ok. I'm staying with my Grandparents in Norfolk until the end of next week, so don't worry about me. I've got a new phone and number to stop Gareth contacting me. Mum's feeling much better. I've told her that you're helping me." Love Daisy

Angela got up and started packing. The girl was safe for now and it wouldn't be long until she was eighteen. At least then, she had options. She was pleased about her friendship with Sarah, although they were young and she was an internet friend, Daisy told her they talked frequently. She was loved and although it didn't make up for having a completely insane stepfather, at least she had someone her own age to talk to.

The tickets were printed. Although Angela knew that there was still a week to go, having everything organised would take some of the pressure off. She felt quite perky after her rest and the news from Daisy helped motivate her. She quickly drove into town to buy some sandals, light summer clothes and sun blocker. She was still tanned from her last trip, but her Marcus and Shaun would need some protection because it was going to be very hot this time of year. While she was walking around the town, she started to wince with pain. She kept forgetting that she hadn't completely healed. She wanted her back to be better by the end of the week, so she better not overdo it. Her neighbour was happy to take over feeding her cat, so there was very little else to worry about, apart from her own level of fitness.

Angela was happy and proud that both Marcus and Shaun had worked so hard. She was sure that they'd achieve good grades. She'd never regarded either of them as particularly academic, just hard workers but now it would seem that anything was possible. It was great that they had so many opportunities ahead of them. She sometimes wished that it was her going to university to start a brand-new career because she needed change.

Angela decided to focus on her shopping and to stop worrying about the future because she knew that it would all work itself out, one way or another. She tried on some white leather sandals, and some summer dresses that she could easily throw over a bikini. She couldn't wait to see Jack again. How could she miss a man that she'd only met for such a short time, but she did. When she went to bed, she thought about them cuddled up on the deck of his yacht looking at the stars. Jack had pointed out the constellations as she snuggled up, with her head resting on his chest. She also remembered the sound of his heart as it rhythmically beat to the gentle waves, which lapped against Virtuous. Virtuous, she smiled. When she was with Jack, she was content just to be in his company. She had no doubt that sex with him would be amazing, but somehow his calm demeanour kept her in a place of wanting to discover more about him. She didn't want to dive into a place of lust. She wanted to know more about his thoughts and feelings, his zest for life. She knew that they'd been in a good place and she hoped that when she returned, they'd still be in that place. Their friendship felt elevated, special and kind. She loved that. Yet he still excited her and she simply couldn't wait to see him again.

Chapter 24 – How did this Happen?

Angela squeezed their suitcases into her car. She planned to drive to Stansted Airport and leave the car in the long stay car park. She knew that it would be expensive to leave it there for six weeks but it was the easiest option.

Marcus and Shaun were very excited. They'd made a plan of the things they wanted to do, and everything was packed, even scuba diving gear. As they left the car and boarded the bus, to the terminal, Angela felt relieved. The time had gone so quickly since they decided to go and she could hardly contain her excitement!

It was a warm day in July and the sky was blue filled with white clouds. It was hot for the UK, so what will it be like in Turkey, she thought. Hopefully not unbearably hot. At least there would be a sea breeze there which always made a difference.

Angela found it boring waiting in airports but for some reason, with reading and her sons playing games on their phones, it seemed like no time at all before they headed for the departure lounge.

"Mum, what's the number of our gate?" asked

Marcus.

"I don't know yet but it will come up soon, so keep an eye out. Not long now until we board," she replied.

"Gate 7," she said suddenly. As Angela walked towards the gate, she said "These airports are massive. There's too much time and then everything's a huge rush."

They got in the queue with their boarding passes at the ready. They knew they'd be seated on the plane quickly because they'd hurried and had passed other people heading in the same direction.

"Mum, why do you keep turning around? We're at the right gate, aren't we?" asked Marcus, who looked worried.

"Yes of course we are. It's just that we are meeting a couple of people who are coming on the trip and if they are not here in a minute, they'll be too late," she said, quietly.

"What," said Marcus.

"Yes, I didn't want to tell you until I was sure, but there a couple of girls coming with us," explained Angela, as diplomatically as possible. But she sensed that their reaction to this sudden news wasn't good.

"I asked Gareth's daughter Daisy and her friend Sarah if they'd like to come with us. I'm sure that they'll do their own thing because they're planning to work in the cafe all summer. I said that they could get the same flight as us so we can travel together. They've never been abroad before," explained Angela.

Marcus and Shaun cringed as a couple of girls came hurtling towards them.

"We thought we'd missed it," said Daisy, whose purple dyed hair flopped over her face.

"No, I would have told them to wait for you," said Angela.

"Hello I'm Sarah," said a tall skinny girl with short hair. She was wearing similar clothes to Daisy but she had numerous ear piercings and a nose stud. Her face appeared to be friendly and she looked happy.

"Hi, I'm Angela and these are my sons Shaun and Marcus," she replied then smiled back.

"Budge up," Sarah suddenly said to Marcus, as she noticed the queue moving. Angela saw a few looks of annoyance from people who lost their place in the queue.

"I can't wait," said Daisy. "I've been so excited. I told Mum I was going with Sarah and she was totally cool about it. To be honest, she was just pleased that I was getting away from Gareth for the whole summer and it's much more exciting than Brighton."

"That's brilliant Daisy. It's fantastic you could come. I hope you told your Mum that you'll both be working?" asked Angela.

"Yeah, I did, but I also told her that we're going to have plenty of fun, aren't we Sarah?" Daisy replied as she gave her friend a little smile. Sarah nodded but she was focusing on keeping her place in the queue.

Marcus and Sean looked away. Angela sensed that they were slightly embarrassed but she then noticed they were also grinning. Finally, they were all seated on the plane. Angela insisted on sitting by the window because she told them that she wanted to look at the clouds. Next to her sat Marcus, then Shaun and Sarah, with Daisy sitting at the end. Everything was pretty quiet and the plane hadn't yet taken off when Angela suddenly received a text from Gareth.

It said: What have you done with Daisy? I can't talk to Linda or my sons now, because she's got an injunction out against me. I need to talk to Daisy because she's been telling lies about me and it's going to look bad when this goes to Court. Do you know where she is Angela? Or shall I come and look for her?

Angela switched off her phone and quickly put it in her bag. She wished that she'd done this before they boarded because she didn't need any more grief. All she wanted to do now was to get to Turkey quickly and safely. She decided that she wouldn't answer him in the future because she now considered him history. This was a new start for her and she wasn't going to let him spoil her happiness. He had brought on his own problems and he deserved it.

"What's the matter Mum, you look upset," asked Shaun, who noticed the expression on her face. Is your back hurting?"

"No, I'm fine, or I will be as soon as we arrive in Turkey," she replied, then smiled at him.

As soon as they arrived at the airport, Angela once again noticed the heat, but she was so thrilled to see

Jean and Alp, she didn't really care.

"It's boiling here," said Shaun turning his cap around to cover his neck.

"Yeah, Mum, you didn't say that it was going to be this hot!" said Marcus.

"As soon as you get in the sea, you'll be fine," said Angela, laughing. "We'll get used to it."

"Yes, come on boys, you don't think about the heat when you're in my pool. It's lovely and cool," said Jean.

It was a little squashed in Jean's car but everyone was too excited to complain. The car flew over the bendy mountain roads with the weight of Jean, the two boys, the girls and Angela. Alp had stayed at the restaurant but he'd told Jean that he'd feed everyone on their arrival.

Everything at the Villa looked bright and clean. Jean had gone to loads of trouble to make up the beds and Angela threw herself on Jean's familiar comfortable sofa. The boys, Daisy and Sarah headed straight to the swimming pool. Jean immediately went to make Angela a cup of tea. She then returned holding two big mugs and sat down next to her.

"Isn't it funny how tea always seems to do the trick even when it comes to extreme heat? I hope you'll soon be feeling better. I can't believe what that monster did to you. You should have gone straight to the Police. When Gareth finds out that his daughter's disappeared with you, he's going to be fuming!" said Jean.

"I know, he's already sent a text but there's

nothing he can do about it because Daisy's eighteen and besides Linda's took an injunction to stop him coming near her and the boys. If he tries to do anything to me or Daisy, it's going to get a lot worse for him. Hopefully, he'll come to realise that he can't control Daisy any longer and give up."

"Let's hope so. What did the boys say, when the girls joined you at the airport? I bet that was a shock for them."

"Yes, it was. They weren't impressed but I didn't want to lie to them. I had to get Daisy out and this was the only thing I could think of. She said that Gareth kept threatening her by text. She's changed her phone but she still didn't feel safe, even at her Grandparents. That's why I suggested she came with us. At first, she refused to come unless Sarah came as well. I decided she could because it would be better for Daisy. Sarah had the money for both fares, so I didn't have to pay for them.

"Well, let's hope that they pull their weight in the bar because Alp is a great guy but when it comes to work, he expects his staff to work very hard," said Jean.

"I'm sure they'll be fine, they're keen enough. Have you seen Jack lately?" asked Angela who wanted to change the subject.

"Ah Jack. He asked me to let him know as soon as you arrive, so I better do that. Every time I see him, he asks about you Ang. When do I think you're coming back? He really thinks a lot of you."

Angela smiled and Jean smiled back. "Why don't

you go and see if he's at the Marina," insisted Jean. I'll keep the youngsters in order. It will make a change for me.

"I don't know. I don't want to pounce on him, the minute I arrive. Although I feel like I do need to stretch my legs. Perhaps I'll go for a run when it cools down a little. I'd love to go for a swim now, if that's ok, before we go down to the restaurant?"

"Yeah, go for it. Alp's still serving lunch and they won't be able to prepare anything for us until about 3ish, anyway. Go and take a splash. I think I'll join you."

Marcus, Shaun and the girls were having great fun playing volleyball in the pool, when Angela plunged into the water. It was surprisingly much cooler than she remembered.

"Ah, that's better. Hey, kids make some space for me. I want to swim a few lengths to cool off," she said. She then swam rapidly up and down the pool, as if she needed to get something out of her system. When she had finished ten lengths, she climbed up the steps and went to sit on a small sun lounger. The sun was still extremely hot and she put her towel around her back to keep warm letting the rest of her body dry in the sun. She then heard Daisy shout, "Hey, Angela, thanks for bringing us. It's fantastic," as she smashed the beach ball with her fist over to Marcus, who laughed and punched it back.

Angela decided to leave going for a run until later because she still felt very tired. She returned to Jean's comfy sofa and soon drifted off to sleep. She was relaxed, happy and relieved that Daisy was safe. After she'd been asleep for about an hour, she suddenly felt her phone vibrate against her leg and realised that someone was calling her. She reached for her phone.

"Angela, where are you? I called at your house earlier to talk about Daisy. I'm still trying to find her. I got into her social media and found messages from this girl from Brighton called Sarah. I guess that's why she wanted to go there. If you know anything about this, you better tell me?"

Angela quickly got up and walked out of the villa. She didn't want Daisy to know that she was speaking to Gareth.

"I don't know where she is! Please don't go to my house because I don't want to be stalked by you?" she said, angrily.

"Stalked! I'm not a stalker but I do think you know where my daughter is. I know you've been talking to her. I called her mobile and it's coming up as an unknown number. I guess she's changed it. Have you got her new number because I need it?"

Angela suddenly realised that Daisy was right behind her.

"Who are you talking to? Is it my dad?" she asked, as she grabbed the phone.

"Gareth, I don't want to see you again. You can stop bullying me because I'm eighteen now. I'm an adult. I fucking hate you. You didn't even remember my birthday. Please leave Angela alone too, because we're in Brighton, for the whole of the summer and we don't know when we'll be back?"

"What, you're in Brighton with Angela?" he shouted loudly!

"Yeah, we're all on holiday and you won't be able to find us. Leave us alone and keep away from Mum too, because she hates you even more than I do," said Daisy.

Daisy passed the phone back to Angela. "Thanks, he'll never find us here because he's stupid," she said.

Angela breathed deeply, got herself together and then went to find Jean who was snoozing by the side of the pool. Her body had turned to a very magnificent shade of brown. Her hair was a lighter shade of blonde and she was clearly enjoying being stretched out in the sun.

"Jean, can we go and find some food now. I'm really hungry and I'd love to show the kids the Marina."

"Yeah sure. I think Alp will be ready for us by now. I hope the kids can cope with the Turkish menu?" said Jean.

"I think Daisy probably can because she's just skewered her father, replied Angela, then started laughing but deep down was worried. She hoped she'd heard the last from Gareth but her intuition told her otherwise!

* * * * *

The meal was delicious and everyone enjoyed it. Alp made Angela's family and the girls feel welcome in the restaurant and there was much laughter around their table. Angela was surprised how well Sarah and Daisy were interacting with her sons. Marcus even told them a little bit about his plans for the future. He was obviously excited about going to Birmingham University. Sarah knew people there, so they managed to find plenty to talk about. Both of her sons were interested in how Sarah ended up in Brighton and the chatting went on and on. Eventually, Angela made an excuse to leave and said she needed to walk. The youngsters decided to stay on at the restaurant because Alp was going to make a start showing them the ropes. Marcus was also interested in doing a little work over the summer.

"Hey Alp, please can I do a few shifts as well, because I want to learn about bar work, in case I need to do it in Birmingham!"

Alp shrugged his shoulders, not really understanding what Marcus said. He then passed him a tea towel and indicated that he could dry some glasses. Angela grinned, waved goodbye to them and headed for the beach. She'd see if Jack was around a little later, once she'd been for a walk. She needed time on her own to think. She walked along the sand stretching out her legs and she began to feel better. She decided to do some simple yoga exercises to rid her of stiffness which had accumulated while she was on the plane. Later, when her food had gone down properly, she'd go for a decent run.

Angela wore a bikini, a pair of joggers and a plain vee neck tee shirt. She looked out to the sea, which was an incredible shade of blue and extremely clear. She decided she'd never be tired of looking at the sea because the beauty of the place was stunning and it made her feel at home. Each wave that rippled on to the shore told its own story. How healing this place was, with its ancient and rugged coastline. There were no lies, no pretense just simple honesty.

Angela sat on the sand absorbing her beautiful surroundings. Her eyes were shut in meditation, embracing a consciousness somewhere between asleep and awake, which allowed her mind to quieten. She very quickly became aware that she could hear another noise, her telephone was ringing again, and once again it was Gareth. She pressed the button to answer and held him away from her ear. She wished she'd ignored it.

"Angela, I warned you and now you can't hold me accountable for what happens." he shouted.

For a moment she was terrified and then it occurred to her. Did she have to go back? Eventually, she'd have to return to her home and cat, but why not stay here. She could find a job. Marcus could come for the holidays and Shaun, well, he'd probably be happy to relocate. The more she thought about it, the more she realised that she didn't want to return to her life in Suffolk, nor to her job at Cherryfields! What she needed was a fresh start. She wanted to break free from her past and wipe the slate clean. She would never tell Gareth where Daisy was because the girl needed protection. Gareth could spend his summer walking around Brighton looking for her if he wanted too, but Daisy was now an adult so she doubted he'd bother. Angela thought that he'd be annoyed for a while then he'd probably give up.

Angela walked to the edge of the water. It was cold, yet refreshing. The waves splashed around her ankles and she gently kicked them, enjoying her freedom. She then realised that Gareth was still ranting down the phone at her, but she'd definitely finished her conversation with him. Without a second thought, Angela then stretched back her arm, so she could no longer hear him. She'd often demonstrated overarm being the most effective way to throw something a distance. It always worked. She took a long deep breath, then quickly threw her phone in the direction of the sea. It became a tiny speck, then a little splash in the vast ocean.

"I'm sorry, but it had to be done," she said. As she went to turn away, she suddenly noticed seven birds hovering where her phone went down. Seagulls looking for fish, thought Angela. As the they flew into the air, she saw they were Magpies!

Angela rubbed her eyes. She must be going mad! Was she having visions? Yet, in a strange way, it felt like confirmation that this part of her life was over. She was free to make a new start. She turned to face the marina and noticed the shape of a very happy balanced and exciting man walking towards her. She smiled and stood still so he could catch her up.

"Angela, I knew you'd return," he said.

"Did you? How could, you be sure?" she replied,

as Jack pulled her close.

"Because you're virtuous. A woman of your word! You knew that I fancied you, and we had fun but I also respect you, Angela. I'm happy to wait until you're ready for me. I've really missed you, but Jean has kept me up to date! But can you please tell me what that splash was about because it looked like you threw something in the water?"

"What splash? Oh, don't ask me about that, because some secrets are best untold," she answered boldly.

"Ok Angela, I won't delve into your secrets because neither of us need complicated," he replied, as he held her hand and suddenly gave it a squeeze.

"I agree, some secrets are best forgotten," she said, smiling.

Chapter 25 – Two weeks later

Angela was pleasantly surprised how well the young people had settled into working at the restaurant. Jean and Alp were impressed by their efforts. Everyone was happy, so she could spend plenty of time with Jack. Over the last few weeks, she'd begun to feel like a different person. Jack was already looking for an apartment for her to rent when she left England. Both of her sons were really happy about the idea. They loved it in Turkey and they were happy to spend more time in such a fabulous place. When they finished their lunchtime shifts, they generally went to the beach, or to the pool to relax. Sometimes, they played pool or darts, with Daisy or Sarah if they were free. The girls didn't often work the same shifts as the lads. It was either Daisy, working with Sarah, or one of the girls working with Marcus and Sean.

Marcus really enjoyed working in the bar and he was surprisingly good at it. He loved talking to people and he was quick on the till. Alp gave them free food and drinks for their trouble, which worked out really well, at least they were self-sufficient. Angela didn't have to find any money for them which made her situation easier.

Yesterday, she'd been on a long trip with Jack and they'd found a beautiful cove not far away. They'd spent the whole day there alone, and they had the most amazing time. She hadn't heard from him today but she knew he planned some serious sailing. She'd told Jean that she'd clean the villa whilst they were working. When she finished, she'd read her book in that amazing hammock!

At 6 pm and feeling slightly hungry, Angela decided that she would go to the restaurant to see how everyone was getting on. She needed to talk to her sons about a few things, but they had disappeared!

"Where have they all gone, Alp?" Angela asked, knowing that they could be busy out the back in the kitchen. They sometimes worked very long hours and she was proud of them. Shaun wasn't old enough to serve behind the bar but he often did jobs to help out in the kitchen. It was hard work for him being only sixteen but he wanted to be included.

"Oh, they gone. They went to swim and play basketball. It's up the road. Sit down and don't worry. Have wine Angela. They be back soon," he said, in broken English which Angela felt was rather cute! She wasn't worried. She took a large swig of wine. It was so wonderful and peaceful here and the people were so friendly. Another bonus was that the drinks and food were cheap. She loved it here. Why would she want to go home to England? There was no need to chase the kids. She'd wait.

Angela suddenly noticed Daisy was sitting in the far corner of the restaurant. She was talking to a man that she'd never seen before. He appeared to be in his forties and quite smartly dressed. He was wearing beige cotton shorts and a loose short-sleeved navy buttoned shirt. He also wore some fashionable shades which were pushed up on his head. They were in deep conversation. She went to introduce herself because she wanted to know who he was. Hopefully he wasn't bothering Daisy? For a few moments, she thought that it could be Gareth and her heart stopped. She walked towards them, casually, so she wouldn't alarm them.

"Hi Daisy, I was looking for Shaun and Marcus. Have you any idea where they are?" she asked.

"Hi Angela, they've gone swimming and to play basketball. They said they'd be back for dinner. I'm glad that you're back from your trip. I want you to meet my dad, John!"

"He's your dad! I don't believe we've met. I'm extremely surprised to meet you here of all places," she said, stretching out her arm to shake John's hand.

"Yeah well, I was surprised too, but found I had a bit of business here. It's nice to meet you, Angela. I've heard so much about you from Daisy. I understand that you brought my daughter and her friend here on holiday. You know, I'm truly grateful you did this. I love my daughter very much and I have to make sure she's happy." he said, smiling.

"It's great that you can spend some time

together," replied Angela, even if it's a long way to come!

"I know, but as I said, I have some business to attend to so I thought that we'd catch up at the same time. It's been a few years since I saw my Mags and she's grown into a really great young woman. I remembered it was her eighteenth birthday. It's been too long but I'm here now. I'm sure that we're going to enjoy the food and sun. What a fabulous restaurant your friends have. I've been working my way through the menu today. I've never eaten such good food," said John.

"Yes, it's fantastic," she replied, smiling at Daisy. So, this was her father. Gareth mentioned him but she got the impression that he was a real waste of space. Perhaps this was another of Gareth's lies because John sounded very down to earth! His voice was slightly gruff, but he was surprisingly polite.

"Well, have fun you two. It's so great to meet you John and I have to say that Daisy looks just like you" she said.

"Yeah, a real chip off the old block," he said, giving Daisy a wink. I'm glad I've finally met you, because I'm only here a few more days then, I need to return to London."

"Ah right, what sort of business are you in?" she asked politely.

"Debt collecting, particularly debts that have gone on for years," he smiled and winked at Daisy before looking Angela straight in the eyes. She gave him a short smile back then turned to walk away. Debt collecting was heavy work so she preferred not to think about it. John's handshake said a lot and her intuition was seldom wrong. Still, Daisy seemed happy enough, that was the main thing.

Angela returned to the apartment and sprawled out on Jean's comfortable sofa. She closed her eyes and slept. She dreamt about the birds she saw on the beach. One minute they were seagulls and the next magpies! She was counting them when she heard a loud bang and jumped up from the sofa.

Jean had walked in through the front door and Alp had slammed it behind her. She didn't look very happy. Alp was telling her that he'd get another one, so don't get upset.

"Get another what?" asked Angela, curiously.

"Alp wants to buy me another ring. He had bought me a ring and hidden it for a surprise. He was going to ask me to marry him on my birthday at the end of the month, but he says that he can't find it anywhere. We're so upset.

Angela went cold. She couldn't believe this. Surely Daisy hadn't taken the ring? Not after everything they'd done for her. But she knew the girl was capable of it. Perhaps she'd been naive and underestimated her. If she had taken it, she was extremely ungrateful.

"Jean, have you and Alp looked everywhere?" she asked in total disbelief.

"Yes, we have. We think that our cleaner may have stolen it. She cleans all the apartments in the block so it could easily be her. It was in that cabinet over there, in the drawer under the drinks part and now it's gone. It took Alp months to save up for it. We are both upset," said Jean who was wiping away her tears.

"We've got to go now. Come on Jean, we'll keep looking and if we can't find it, I'll buy you another one. We're still going to get married" said Alp, giving her a squeeze. They both walked out of the door and headed back to the restaurant together. As they walked down the path, Angela heard Jean mutter that she felt someone must have stolen it, and it was best to report it.

Angela felt really upset. She didn't dare say anything to Jean about Daisy's stealing. She had no evidence it was her, so she didn't want to point the finger at her until she was completely sure. She strode into the bedroom where the girls were staying. It was very untidy. The bed was unmade and the bed covers were strewn all over the floor. There were also piles of clothes everywhere. Didn't they tidy up, she thought, feeling exasperated! Some of the drawers to their dressing tables were open and there were suitcases half pushed under the bed. Angela didn't know where to start to look for the ring. She felt bad invading the girls' privacy but she had to know that neither of them had taken the ring. As she began to search, her heart pounded because they could return and find her going through their things. The last thing that she wanted to do, was to get into an argument with Daisy, especially in front of her sons. Accusing Daisy of stealing now could prove fatal because she would likely fly off the handle when she was just beginning to find her feet.

She searched their bathroom, the chest of drawers and all the places she could think of. The only place that she hadn't searched, were the suitcases. She quickly pulled out a small black suitcase, which she presumed belonged to Daisy. It had several pockets which could be unzipped. They were all empty except one, which felt like it had something rattling in it. Angela plunged her hand into the pocket and felt what seemed to be her passport and watch. There was definitely no engagement ring, but decided to pull out the watch and passport to double check the compartment. To her horror, the passport fell open to reveal a picture of Gareth. Angela quickly realised it was his and then noticed watch was big too big for Daisy, so it must also be his! With her heart pounding, she decided to re-check the other pockets. Very soon her hand laid on something that felt like a mobile. It was Daisy's old mobile, the one that she said was no longer used! Angela turned it on. There was only one bar of battery left. Fortunately, Daisy hadn't deleted the text messages, so she could still read them.

Hi Daisy, we need to chat. I'm arriving at Dalaman Airport on Tuesday afternoon. I'll meet you there. Don't tell anyone I called you. When I text, get a taxi to the airport and I'll meet you in arrivals. I've put some money in your bank account. We need to sort a few things out because your real dad's been threatening me. He says I owe him money. You need to come back to England with me so we can have a proper chat about him. Don't tell Angela or Jean that I'm coming to get you, or there'll be real trouble. I know exactly where you are because Angela's neighbours told me about Turkey. It didn't take long to find out where you're staying. I told the police about the jewellery from the market and they want to talk to you, so you'll have to come back with me, Gareth.

Angela scrolled down to look at the rest of the sent messages. Some of them were extremely long and went into two messages.

Hi Dad, Gareth's threatening me and says he's coming to take me back to England. I don't want to go. I'm scared of what he'll do to me. Please come soon. Love Daisy x

Angela noticed that the dates of the messages were several days ago. Then, she saw that there was another text, this time from John.

Mags don't worry, I'll sort it. Just let me know the date, time and flight he's on. I know how to deal with people like him. It was difficult in England, because of your Mum, but it's a lot easier here. I'll meet him instead of you. That'll surprise him. Dad x

Angela looked at the passport and watch in her hand. The engagement ring no longer felt important. She rapidly put the passport and the watch into the rear pocket, of Daisy's case. She needed to think about the way to handle this. She was horrified. What did John mean by he'd deal with it? Where had Gareth gone? Perhaps he was already here! The thought of that man being anywhere within the vicinity of the villa sent a shiver down her spine. He obviously intended to come but she hadn't seen him. Daisy must know something about this, why else would there be his passport and watch in her suitcase. Something had been going on here that she knew nothing about. This was terrible. She'd have to confront Daisy about the ring, watch and passport but it wouldn't be easy.

As soon as Angela had zipped up the case, she looked up and saw that Daisy was standing at the bedroom door, staring. Her terrified face said it all.

"Daisy, what happened? I found Gareth's passport and watch in your suitcase and I've read the messages on your old phone. The one you said, you didn't use?" questioned Angela passing her the mobile.

Daisy stood there flabbergasted and just stared at her for several minutes.

"Ok, I'll tell you about it but can you keep a secret?" she asked, with a straight face.

"Yes, of course I can," replied Angela, as she started to feel annoyed.

"It depends on what?"

"No Daisy, not, it depends on what! I can keep a secret, whatever it is. So, you better tell me what's been going on because it must be something serious," asked Angela.

"Well, you know that Gareth's not my real Dad, don't you?" she continued.

"Yes, of course, I know that. Gareth told me and I

met John the other day when you were with him." said Angela who now felt on the verge of explosion!

"Well, you know that I collect jewellery and things."

"Yes," she replied, wondering where this was going.

"Well, Dad says he didn't see me much because he's been collecting things as well, for years. He's got an even bigger nest than me. He collects all sorts, even people," said Daisy, innocently.

"Really, that doesn't surprise me", Angela whispered as she tried to keep calm. The bottom of the nest went far deeper than she imagined. Perhaps John had been secretly setting up Daisy for a life of crime.

"Only bad people and not many. Those who refuse to pay their debts. My dad named me Magpie because he started my collection when I was a baby and he's been sending me jewellery ever since. Gareth doesn't know why I had so much and I've never told him. Gareth owes Dad loads of money and he let him down badly. He was a very bad person," she said, with no remorse.

"He was, a really bad person! What does that mean? I can keep a secret, Daisy. You have to tell me what's been going on and you have to give the ring back," she said, hoping that this would bring out more of the truth.

"Oh, the ring, I'm wearing it. I was going to keep it, then I realised that Jean and Alp are really lovely people and I wanted to put it back but I couldn't find the right time to do it without them realising what I'd done! Can you give it back, please Angela?" said Daisy, looking at her with a strange twinkle in her eye.

Angela sighed. It was going to be difficult because she'd have to explain Daisy's behaviour and why the girl was compelled to steal jewellery! She was going to be cross and it might compromise them staying at the villa.

"Well," she said, feeling as if she had little choice but to help.

"Thanks Angela. You're great. I'm really happy I met you, Marcus and Shaun. Marcus also helped us when we couldn't move the body," said Daisy, unexpectedly.

"Marcus helped you move Gareth. Oh my God. No, you're not telling me the truth are you, Daisy? Marcus would never do something like that. He doesn't know John. He's never met him so why would he help?"

"He would do that. He told me he hated Gareth because he'd been to your house and threatened him. He said, he's a really nasty piece of work and he didn't understand why you couldn't see what he was like. He didn't want to help at first but when I explained about the golf club, he wanted to help to make sure that he never went near you again."

Marcus suddenly breezed into the lounge in his shorts and tee shirt. He looked surprisingly fit after a long shift in the restaurant, playing basketball and then swimming. It was extremely hot, so he flopped down on the sofa next to Daisy.

"Alright Mags? Fancy a game of volleyball later?" he asked, smiling at her.

"Yeah ok, in a while. I've been telling Angela how you helped Dad and I lift Gareth into that box because we couldn't do it on our own," she replied, grinning.

"Daisy. For Christ's sake! You were told to keep it a secret. What the hell are you doing? You know I didn't want to be involved. I only agreed to help because you persuaded me. Although the guy was way out of control." replied Marcus, who was raging.

"What do you mean, out of control?" asked Angela, horrified.

"Well, you may as well know now Mum. Gareth came around to our house asking for you one evening, when you were out. He said he was going to fucking murder you if you kept interfering in his life. I said you weren't here and he said, make sure you stay away. He then grabbed me around the neck and flung me against the hallway wall. He put his fist right up to my face. I didn't know that you were still seeing him because you told us it was over. He was a real game player. A nasty piece of work. He was setting you up for something horrible. I didn't know what was going on with you two but after you came back hardly able to walk and in terrible pain, I realised that something bad had happened. I decided the best thing to do was to do a little bit of investigating myself before I said anything. I found out that he was never an architect, that was a load of bull! He was a partner in some debt collecting firm in London and he went bankrupt."

"What, you knew all this about him. Why didn't you tell me?"

"I've only just found some of it out because John filled in the gaps. Apparently, they were in partnership together and Gareth did the dirty on him. He kept stealing money from the business because he had a gambling habit. In the end, he bankrupted it."

"But Gareth is dead! Does Shaun know anything about this?"

"No, of course not. He was out when Gareth turned up. I didn't dare tell you either. I wanted to protect you, Mum. I thought you were over. I was going to deal with it myself, but I did the wrong not telling you. I was so ashamed when you came home in terrible pain. Gareth wasn't dead, although he looked it. I think John gave him a good hiding but he was still moving. I helped John and Daisy with his body because there was no-one else to do it!" continued Marcus as he angrily strode around the room. I think John wanted to shake him up a bit but I'm sure he wasn't dead.

Daisy suddenly took off the engagement ring and laid it on the coffee table. Angela looked at it and realised the only thing that she could do was to come clean and tell Jean the truth. It was difficult because Daisy obviously couldn't help herself. For some reason, the girl felt that she had a right to any jewellery she was dawn too. It was a fascination which Angela concluded was through her lack of self-love. Angela sighed and reminded herself that not everything in life was black and white. There were definitely some shades of grey and she was constantly finding them. She stood there looking at them unsure what to say. Then she randomly said,

"Can you believe I saw seven Magpies today hovering over the sea? At first, I thought they were seagulls, but they changed before my eyes. It was the strangest experience I've ever had. I still don't know if it was real. Now you tell me this, I must be going mad seeing and hearing things beyond belief. The pair of them sat side by side on the sofa. They were good friends now and they looked as if they were waiting for some sort of answer. She took a long deep breath and stared out of the window. If there was an answer to this, it certainly wasn't an easy one. She needed a miracle.

Angela suddenly heard Jack behind her. She had no idea how long he'd been standing there and she waited for him to speak.

"They're right Angela. Gareth isn't dead. Although the guy thought he was dead being left in a box all night in the harbour. I was woken up very early this morning to the sound of this banging against the side of Virtuous. I could believe it when I saw this huge wooden box and what sounded like muffled cries coming from it. I managed to steady it and eventually with the help of a couple of friends we managed to get it open. There stood a very wet and thoroughly confused man who said that he thought his name was Gareth, although to be honest, I'm not entirely sure he knows who he is anymore. He kept asking for you Angela. I have no idea how long he'd been in the box. It could have been a night or several days. I gave him some old clothes and he's waiting for us on Virtuous. I locked him in the cabin. He's very lucky he didn't drown, but the box appeared to be watertight. He was starving though, so I gave him some food.

"I don't want to see him, Jack. He tried to ruin my life, as well as abusing Daisy and her mother. He's a very violent man. We ought to get in touch with the police," said Angela as her heart began to race.

"The Police come here? No, I don't think that's a good idea. I know all about his past because John told me what's been going on and the man needs help. I'm a little shocked that you didn't tell me about him though, especially what he did to you? At least I know now. I think the best plan is for all of us to go and talk to him," suggested Jack.

"Yes, I want to see him and make sure that he never bothers any of us again," said Daisy.

"I don't think he'll be doing that, because he's absolutely petrified and to be honest, he's also weak."

"Okay, let's go and get it over and done with," said Angela.

They all left together. Marcus walked alongside Daisy, and Angela walked with Jack. They left a note for Shaun to say they'd be back soon. Angela was pleased Jack was with her because as they stepped on to Virtuous, she suddenly felt calm. For the first time in a long time, she no longer felt vulnerable. She could be strong with Gareth and it was time to speak her truth. As Jack unlocked the cabin, Daisy suddenly pushed through the door to reach him.

"Daisy, I'm so sorry for what I've done. I realise I was cruel and abusive to your mother and I bullied you. I wanted to keep the boys and I was scared of losing them."

"Gareth, you know that's not true. Mum was nothing but kind to you, and you and your rich friends at the club, enjoyed making her suffer. You made our lives hell! We've decided not to call the Police but we want you to go back to England and leave us alone, or we'll tell the truth about what you did to us! I now have Angela as a witness," said Daisy staring him right in the eyes.

"Oh yes Angela, little miss, I have to look after everyone."

"Yes, Angela, and she's taken better care of me than you ever did. I've brought your passport, phone and keys, so you can leave now but you'll have to walk because I've taken your money."

"A Magpie to the end, eh Daisy," he mumbled sarcastically. As Gareth stood up to leave, he picked up his keys and glanced in his wallet to check his money. He then turned to face Daisy and simply said, "You're definitely your father's daughter. You were never mine. I only had you because your mother couldn't cope."

Daisy stared at him defiantly "Yes, I'm a Magpie to the end."

John stood on the Jetty waiting for them. He saw Gareth leave but said nothing. His daughter had said it all.

"Well done, Mags, I heard what you said. You were stronger than I thought. When you come back to England, you can come and live with me and your friend can too, if she wants to. I live in a big house now, so there's loads of space. Mind you if your hoard gets any bigger?" said John, laughing.

"Really that's cool! Can I invite whoever I want?"

"That's not a problem," said John but I want you to apologise to Jean and Alp for stealing their ring! You've still got a lot to learn," he said, giving Angela a wink.

"Thank God for that," said Jack, as he saw them walking away.

"Yes, but I hope Gareth keeps away," said Angela.

"I don't think he'll be back but it's best we don't mention this to anyone," said Jack, especially not to the Police!

"But what would Virtuous make of that?" asked Angela.

"Oh, I reckon she'd approve."

"Really?" she whispered and smiled.

"Yes, because life's a journey," replied Jack.

"I like my journey," she said.

ABOUT THE AUTHOR

Jennifer Lynch lives in Norfolk. She's a keen walker animal lover and dancer. She started writing to keep her busy in the evenings when she was a single parent and didn't have a life! She now works as an empowerment coach and reiki healer, writer and poet. Her books include The Silver Lining, William's Wishes, Liberty Angel, Never to be Told, Salsa, We Hear You Angels and eBooks 5th Dimensional Earth and Attracting What You Really Want.

She can be contacted via her website www.angelwisdom.co.uk